Captain Butcher's Body

Books by Scott Corbett

The Trick Books

THE LEMONADE TRICK
THE MAILBOX TRICK
THE DISAPPEARING DOG TRICK
THE LIMERICK TRICK
THE BASEBALL TRICK
THE TURNABOUT TRICK
THE HAIRY HORROR TRICK
THE HATEFUL PLATEFUL TRICK
THE HOME RUN TRICK
THE HOCKEY TRICK
THE BLACK MASK TRICK

Suspense Stories

COP'S KID
TREE HOUSE ISLAND
DEAD MAN'S LIGHT
CUTLASS ISLAND
ONE BY SEA
THE BASEBALL BARGAIN
THE MYSTERY MAN
DEAD BEFORE DOCKING
RUN FOR THE MONEY
THE CASE OF THE GONE GOOSE
THE CASE OF THE FUGITIVE
    FIREBUG

THE CASE OF THE TICKLISH
    TOOTH
THE CASE OF THE SILVER SKULL
THE CASE OF THE BURGLED
    BLESSING BOX

Easy-to-read Adventures

DR. MERLIN'S MAGIC SHOP
THE GREAT CUSTARD PIE PANIC
THE BOY WHO WALKED ON AIR
THE GREAT MCGONIGGLE'S
    GRAY GHOST
THE GREAT MCGONIGGLE'S
    KEY PLAY

What Makes It Work?

WHAT MAKES A CAR GO?
WHAT MAKES A TV WORK?
WHAT MAKES A LIGHT GO ON?
WHAT MAKES A PLANE FLY?
WHAT MAKES A BOAT FLOAT?

Ghost Stories

THE RED ROOM RIDDLE
HERE LIES THE BODY
CAPTAIN BUTCHER'S BODY

Captain Butcher's Body

Scott Corbett

Illustrated by Geff Gerlach

An Atlantic Monthly Press Book

Boston   Little, Brown and Company   Toronto

FIRST EDITION

T 10/76

Library of Congress Cataloging in Publication Data

Corbett, Scott.
  Captain Butcher's body.

  "An Atlantic Monthly Press book."
  SUMMARY: Two boys confront the ghost of a
long-dead pirate on an island off the coast of
New England.
  [1. Pirates—Fiction. 2. Ghost stories]
I. Gerlach, Geff. II. Title.
PZ7.C79938Caj   [Fic]   76-28453
ISBN 0-316-15727-9

ATLANTIC—LITTLE, BROWN BOOKS
ARE PUBLISHED BY
LITTLE, BROWN AND COMPANY
IN ASSOCIATION WITH
THE ATLANTIC MONTHLY PRESS

*Published simultaneously in Canada
by Little, Brown & Company (Canada) Limited*

PRINTED IN THE UNITED STATES OF AMERICA

To Eleanor, Harry, and Barbara Callahan,
best of neighbors

Captain Butcher's body
Shall never lie at rest;
Doomed is he each century
To repeat his bloody jest!

— Prisoners' jingle
reported by
Warder Higby, 1746

1

Leo's Ghost

One

Books can be time bombs.

A book can sit quietly on a shelf for years and years. Then someone takes the book from the shelf and opens it and reads a chapter . . . and, like an explosion, the book's contents change a lot of things that once seemed unshakable.

Sitting on a shelf in an old-fashioned bookcase with glass-paneled doors, in an old-fashioned house on Broadmoor Island, was a book called *Ghosts of the New England Coast*. It had been sitting there for years, untouched. It was still there the day before we arrived.

But by the time we got there, the book had been taken out and opened.

All this happened long ago, the year after World War II ended, when I was eleven years old. Of course, it wasn't just the book. There was also something an old gentleman had once told me; there was Marshall Watkins, and Mr. Whitney; there was a small, deserted cove, and a rough stone tower . . . And there was Leo. There were all these elements, coming together.

Coming together on Broadmoor Island.

"Leo!" A chance reminder of my cousin Leo had set my father off all over again. "I don't know whether I can take a whole summer of Leo or not. That last time —"

"Now, Paul . . ."

Mom's eyes flicked in my direction. That was supposed to remind him that he should not criticize a relative when young ears were around. But as usual he was hard to control.

"All the same, Carol, that summer was a madhouse, and young Leo put the frosting on the cake. Of all the pompous little whippersnappers —"

"Well, he's four years older now . . ."

"Four years worse," I predicted.

"That will be enough out of you, young man."

"But, Mom, how am *I* supposed to stand a whole summer of Leo?"

Of course, we had a nerve to complain about anything, even Cousin Leo. There we were on the deck of the mailboat, dancing across little blue waves off the New England coast, bound for an island where a lot of people would have given their eyeteeth to spend the summer. Which was exactly the view my mother took of the matter.

4

"George Crowell, are you eleven years old, or eleven months? For heaven's sake, I don't know which one of you is the biggest baby, but you're both impossible." She turned to my father. "Now, look, Paul. You've been through a great deal. Nothing will be better for you than to have some fresh air and peace and quiet — now, don't interrupt! With the girls away at camp there will only be six of us in that great big house. There's plenty of space for you to have a room to work in where nobody will bother you. I think it was lovely of your Aunt Fanny to invite us. It's just the place for you to get back to work on your book. What is more, if you don't stop looking like an early Christian martyr I'm going to hit you with something heavy!"

"And make me a *real* Christian martyr," said Dad, brightening up.

"Besides, you're forgetting one thing that will make all the difference. Last time Aunt Fanny wasn't on hand to keep order!"

That was true, of course. Aunt Fanny had been off in the middle of Maine nursing her elder sister Nellie back to health. Just when we had needed a firm hand at the tiller she had been denied to us. But all that was past history. Now, four summers later, my father had returned. He had been away for nearly all of those four years helping to win World War II.

In civilian life he was a university professor of Asiatic history. Army Intelligence had sent him to China shortly after our stay at Aunt Fanny's — and after that summer he had almost been glad to go. When he left he had been working on a book about

China's maritime history. Now he was anxious to get back to work on it.

Fortunately, before Mom was forced to hit either of us with something heavy our conversation was interrupted. Someone had sighted Broadmoor. I jumped up and ran forward to the bow for a look. My parents followed.

"Sure enough, there she lies. Devil's Island," said my father, still asking for trouble.

"Where?"

"Dead ahead."

It took my unpracticed eyes a moment to pick up the low blur that smudged the horizon.

"How soon will we be there?"

"On this stout craft of ours, in about an hour."

The launch that ran out to Broadmoor in those days was a sturdy, broad-beamed old tub that could carry a hundred passengers if she had to, but she seldom had to. Our island — I think of it that way now — our small island did not attract many tourists. There was no car ferry to take your own car on, and only two or three taxis to be had when you got there.

Cars of any kind were few out there, in fact, and except in Newgate, the only town on the island, there was nothing but sandy dirt roads to drive them on. One or two weatherbeaten old summer hotels and a couple of gift shops were the island's major concessions to the summer complaints, as off-island visitors were called.

The launch made two round trips a day. In the

morning she was referred to as the mailboat because she brought the mail. On her second run she was referred to as the afternoon boat. The same boat both times, mind you, but that was the way we made it clear which run we were referring to.

After a while my parents sat down again on a nearby bench while I lingered at the rail. In spite of the crosswind that blew some of their words away, a few snatches of their conversation reached my ears.

"— and Gladys, for Pete's sake —"

"Now, Paul . . ."

"What Frank ever saw in that —"

The wind took his next word, but I supplied it for myself. Birdbrain! I thought with a grin, having heard Dad use that word once before to describe Aunt Gladys.

"Yes, dear," Dad was presently saying, after a short but lively lecture from my mother, by which time I had edged down the rail, "but you know very well Gladys thinks her Leo is the family genius and can do no wrong. I'll bet he does whatever he pleases."

"I wouldn't worry about that out here, Paul. Nobody's going to get away with anything as long as Aunt Fanny's around. She'll have us all toeing the line — and that will include you as well as Leo. I can hardly wait!"

Dad snorted.

"Well, yes, thank heaven for Aunt Fanny. She —"

"George!"

"Huh? Oh — hi, Mom!"

"George Crowell, are you being pitcher ears again?"

"Who, me? Heck no, Mom, I didn't hear a thing you said about Aunt Gladys and Leo and Aunt Fanny!"

She tweaked my ear and told me to sit down.

"Don't pay any attention to the things your father says. We all know he's a first-class stinker."

"You shouldn't talk that way about a relative, Mom."

"He's no kin of mine, I only married him!" she pointed out, while Dad clapped me on the knee. He was beginning to feel better. Glancing ahead at the smudge on the horizon, he subsided into a gentler mood.

"Four years! That's a long time. You were only seven then, George. And the twins were twelve."

My twin sisters were sixteen now and had jobs for the summer as camp counselors.

"I'll bet Leo was glad when he heard Nan and Linda weren't coming, huh, Dad?"

Enough of gentler moods! Dad's eyes fired up again with the light of battle and he snickered savagely.

"We'll threaten to send for them if he steps out of line. How well do you remember that summer, George?"

"Pretty well. But one thing I remember best of all."

"What's that, son?"

As if he didn't know. Even Mom had to laugh as I gave the expected answer.

"Leo's Ghost!"

Two

Leo's Ghost. Yes, indeed, we all remembered Leo's Ghost, from that summer before World War II when I was seven. We had only been at Aunt Fanny's for two weeks when Cousin Leo and Aunt Gladys showed up, and by then Aunt Fanny had been called away to her sister's bedside. She had left us with great misgivings, sensing that our two families might get into trouble when left on our own without a higher authority — herself — on hand to settle squabbles.

My Uncle Frank, a naval officer, had been killed in action at Pearl Harbor, leaving behind a young widow with one child, my cousin Leo. Aunt Gladys was just the sort of silly, ineffectual, timid soul well calculated to irritate my father. As for Leo — well, you'll see.

Even then we might have scraped by without any

major blowups if my sisters had only gone off to camp that year instead of coming along. What a pair! They were not to be trusted. I know. Older sisters of any kind can be bad enough at times, but when they are twins, and twins who love pranks, Little Brother is liable to have an eventful childhood.

When I was not walking around with a Kick Me sign stuck on my back, I was finding what felt like snakes in my bed or what definitely was a toad in my lunchbox.

The trouble with twins is, their teamwork is often devastating. They always seem to know what each other is thinking. Give a pair like that a roughhouse sense of humor and no one is safe.

Just such a pair were my sisters Linda and Nancy.

Dad drove down in the old touring car to meet the afternoon boat. If Aunt Fanny had been there she would have been driving. She never let anyone else touch the wheel when she was in the car. She was small and slim, but she sat tall in the saddle when driving. The very way she gripped the wheel was enough to let any car know who was boss.

The twins and I had a noisy three-way argument about who would get to go with Dad. He solved this neatly by leaving us all home.

"If they have much luggage there won't be room for you coming back, anyway," he said. Touring cars did not have trunks.

We were all waiting in the front yard when the car chugged back up the hill from the harbor, and I can still see Leo, ten years old then, sitting in the back seat with a canvas suitcase on his lap and his arms around each side of it, guarding it from the world. Piled in beside him were enough parcels and bags and suitcases to account for the look on my father's face.

Leo was a pudgy boy with a large head that seemed even larger because of the way his forehead bulged. Below the ponderous forehead brooded a deep-set pair of dark eyes separated by an insignificant nose. His small mouth had rather full lips which he had a habit of pursing and pushing out in a way that made him look insufferably smug.

His voice was high and reedy, his speech precise. He chose his words with the fussy deliberation some people display when making a selection from a box of assorted chocolates. To hear that fluting voice fashioning bookish sentences was enough to set anyone's teeth on edge.

There was the usual confusion of greetings as we all kissed Aunt Gladys and said hello to Leo, and everyone helped with the luggage.

"Hey, what's this?" asked Nan, lifting out a bundle of poles and a tarp. You going camping, Leo?"

The full lips pursed and pushed.

"I plan to sleep in my pup tent in the yard, so that I can be up early for birdwatching," he announced. "Never mind, I'll take that," he added sharply as Linda picked up the canvas suitcase he had set carefully to one side.

"Okay by me — it weighs a ton," said Linda.

11

"What's in it, a rock collection?"

"My field glasses are in it, and they're very expensive, and also some books I'm using for research."

"Bird books?"

"No — well, a couple of field guides, but —"

Aunt Gladys put her head on one side and looked pretty much like a bird herself.

"Leo is always deep into something," she said in worshipful tones. "Right now he's researching psychic phem — phen —"

"Psychic phenomena, Mother," snapped Leo, and of course that jarred on us. We were at the stage when any kid who called his mother "Mother" was putting on airs.

"Leo likes to read ghost stories," Dad translated, and got himself an annoyed look from Leo.

"Not ghost *stories*, Uncle Paul, I'm digging into actual case histories. And I haven't made up my mind yet what to believe."

I know Leo sounds impossible, and he was, and yet there was no escaping the impression of precocious intelligence brooding in dark corners, operating on a level far beyond his years. The mind behind those deep-set eyes was an instrument of undeniable power, restless and probing. Still, he *was* impossible, and when I caught the twins looking at each other I knew at once what they were thinking.

They were thinking about ways and means of sawing Cousin Leo down to size.

When all the luggage had been taken inside and

Dad and Mom were helping Aunt Gladys get settled the twins drifted away to the backyard. I tagged along.

Leo had already carried his tenting equipment around the side of the house and dumped it in a corner of the backyard. Not far from his proposed tent site tall lilac bushes formed hedges bordering a wide path that ran back to a rectangular clearing. At the head of the clearing a clothesline stretched across in front of a big vegetable garden. The two poles that held the line were set far enough apart so that they did not show when you looked down the path. The clothesline was a double one, and ran through pulleys attached to the poles so that the line could be pulled back and forth.

Linda examined the knot in the clothesline.

"Easy," she murmured. "And when it's undone there will be plenty to let down to the ground . . ."

Nan ran the line back and forth a few feet.

"The pulleys don't squeak much . . ."

"And the chains will take care of that . . ."

"What are you going to do?" demanded Little Brother.

They gave me a thoughtful glance.

"You can help," Linda decided. "You can stand guard while we're in the attic."

"In the attic? When?"

"Later. Come on, Nan, let's go over to the barn and see about chains."

After dinner that night everyone was sitting out on the veranda having what Aunt Fanny would have called "a nice visit." Mom and Aunt Gladys were doing most of the talking, though Dad did make a manly effort to think of a few things to say to Aunt Gladys. And I would not want to give the wrong impression here for one minute. Dad did not dislike Aunt Gladys. He merely thought she was an idiot.

When I said everyone was on the veranda I should have said everyone but Leo. Leo was busy in the backyard pitching his pup tent. By the time he had arranged everything to his niggling satisfaction and returned to the veranda, dusk was settling under the trees and wisps of gray were moving like clammy fingers.

"Fog's going to come in pretty thick tonight," commented Dad, casting an experienced eye around the yard. "Sure you want to sleep out there, Leo?"

Leo's arrogance often made the simplest retorts offensive even when the words seemed innocuous. It was so now as he replied, "I don't mind a little fog, Uncle Paul."

"We're not talking about a little fog, Leo, we're talking about a lot of fog." Nettled by Leo's contemptuous tone of voice, Dad was goaded into creating what turned out to be a monumental misunderstanding, one of those ill-timed remarks around which family feuds can lovingly twine for decades, given the chance.

"However . . . if it's spooks you're after, Leo, you'll find it spooky enough out there tonight."

"Spooky!" Almost jeeringly, Leo shook his head in a pitying way over the word, which he seemed to consider childish.

14

"Okay, Leo. You've had fair warning," said Dad, making it worse.

"I've never seen a more fearless boy than Leo," said his adoring parent.

"Oh, Mother!"

"Well, it's true."

Through all of this I could feel the beady eyes of my sisters on me and I knew it would be worth my life to giggle, so I didn't. But the way Dad had innocently mentioned spooks seemed so hilarious at the time I could hardly stand it. Little did we know what we were letting him in for.

When they were hatching a plot the twins thought of everything. Almost everything, anyway. At least, they were on the ball where I was concerned. Otherwise, when Mom announced my bedtime I would probably have marched off without a murmur, which might have been fatal.

"You stay in your room tonight and don't make a sound," Linda had ordered. "Your room is perfect for seeing everything and giving us the signal."

I giggled wildly.

"Gee, I can't wait!"

"You darn well *better* wait, if you know what's good for you," said Nan grimly. "Don't jump up and take off tonight the second Mom says it's your bedtime. Complain a little, the same as usual, or she's liable to get suspicious that something's going on. You know *her!*"

"Yeah," sighed Linda, "she's a deep one!"

So when the time came I was ready.

"Aw, Mom, do I have to go to bed *now,* when everybody else gets to stay up?"

"Everybody else is a good deal older than you are, George."

"Leo's only ten!"

"Which is nearly fifty percent older than you are," said Leo in a lofty tone of voice. He looked at his watch. "Anyway, you don't have to whine on account of me. I'm going to turn in soon myself, because I'll be up at dawn."

Proud of my performance, I grumbled a good night to everyone and went up to my room. The instant I reached it I flew out of my clothes into my pajamas and grabbed my flashlight, which had already been outfitted and tested by the girls. It had a piece of red tissue paper over the end of it, held in place by a rubber band.

I wanted to make sure I had the button set just right, but naturally I couldn't simply stand in the middle of the room and try it. That would not have been cloak-and-daggerish enough to suit me at such a time. No, I crawled under the bed before touching the button.

The red end glowed for a split second in a most satisfactory way. I was ready. Crawling out again I posted myself at the window and eagerly surveyed the creepy scene outside.

Three

We could not have asked for a better night. Wisps of fog curled and swirled across the backyard, and yet the darkness was far from total because somewhere up above the fog a bright moon was shining.

Have you ever seen fog on a night when the moon is almost full? Moonlight gives it a luminous, almost phosphorescent, quality that makes it even eerier than fog on a really dark night.

Leo's tent was a dark patch on the lawn, the straight path to the vegetable garden was a pale, glowing strip between the towering hedges, the garden itself a grotto in the fog. It was an enchanted scene in which nothing moved but those slow whorls of gray mist.

Time passes slowly for a seven-year-old. After a while it seemed to me the porch crowd was going to sit around down there forever. I even began to rub my eyes, but the horrible thought of falling asleep at my post was enough to jerk me awake again. Just when I was beginning to wonder if it would be sinful to pray for people to go to bed, I heard Aunt Gladys speak up.

"Well, if you'll excuse me, I guess I'd better turn in. It's been a long day."

Dad was quick to respond to this good news.

"It's bed and a book for me, too," he said heartily, and I could hear him enjoying a big yawn, making the most of it.

Aunt Gladys spoke to Leo in that way we quickly came to hate — almost an apologetic whine, as though she hoped he would not resent her making a suggestion.

"Leo, dear, you really should go to sleep, too, if you're going to get up at dawn — what a horrible thought! Have you got your flashlight?"

"Yes, but I won't need it, Mother." Despite all his talk about turning in early he was still there, which would have annoyed me greatly in ordinary circumstances. "A flashlight doesn't do any good in fog. It hardly penetrates at all."

Penetrates! Even then, when he was ten, Leo was always using words like that in ordinary conversation.

"Besides, I can see my tent perfectly well from here. Can't you see it, Mother?"

"Well, yes, I guess I can. But I wouldn't *think* of walking out there all alone!"

"Oh, Mother!"

There was a general stir down on the veranda — chairs scraping, the rattle of things being gathered up to take into the house, the scuff of footsteps from outside to inside. I could hear Leo say he was going to fill his canteen.

Under the bed went the flashlight, into the bed went Little Brother, ready for a bed check, knowing it would come. Footsteps creaked up the stairs, low-voiced good nights were spoken in the hall, doors opened and closed. My own door was quietly opened. A shaft of light from the hall fell across the bed and registered on my tightly shut eyelids as I went into my Sleeping Angel routine (according to parents, even the worst kids look angelic when they are asleep). My pose must have been convincing, because after a few seconds the door softly closed again and I was left in darkness.

I waited until I heard my mother's footsteps go down the hall, then popped out of bed again, reaching the window in time to see what I had hoped to see. A fuzzy figure was moving slowly through the wisps of fog across the lawn. Leo was on his way to his tent.

Retrieving my flashlight I took up my post at the window.

Now a new period of waiting began. After all, some time had to be allowed for everybody to settle down.

Fortunately the grown-ups' rooms were all on the front of the house. Leading to the kitchen were back stairs down which bare feet could steal without a sound. Even though my room was close to those stairs and I knew two pairs of feet would be traveling them sooner or later, I never heard them.

The peace and quiet of nighttime filled the house. Snug and secure at my window, I stared out into a luminous darkness where the lawn was laid away in shrouds of fog, where an owl hooted and something stirred now and then in the brush, and I wondered how Leo really felt, alone in his small dark tent.

How much longer? Once more time was shuffling its feet and hanging around like an unwanted guest. Once again I was rubbing my eyes . . .

And then I was wide awake and straining my eyes and ears.

What was that funny noise?

A groan or a moan, it was hard to say. Nothing crude, nothing overdone. Just enough of a sound to make anyone wonder what could be making it.

My eyes were on the dark triangular blob of canvas on the lawn, my thumb poised above the flashlight button. Something stirred down there. A pudgy lump separated itself from the blob. Leo had crawled out of the tent. He was a vague form now, turned toward the path between the lilac bushes, with his back toward me. My thumb twitched.

The quick wink of the flashlight seemed like a red blaze. It startled me so I almost dropped the flashlight. Surely Leo would whirl around to see what had caused the whole landscape to light up! That was what I thought, not realizing how dimly the red spot would

show through the fog. When Leo gave no sign of having noticed I was astonished, and began to breathe again.

But had anyone else seen my signal?

A louder moan answered this question. A moan, and then, down at the far end of the path, something began to rise from the ground.

At first it might have been part of the fog itself, but then it became whiter and took form, and seemed to wave a pair of arms as it bounced up and down in the air, then began to move to one side and return, as though walking or gliding back and forth, with more moans and a rattle of chains accompanying its ghostly progress.

If I had been Leo I know what I would have done. I would have let out a yell that would have carried to the mainland and I would have lit out for the house at a pace no mere streak of lightning could have thought of matching. In other words, I would have done exactly what we expected Leo to do.

But instead, what was he doing? Was I seeing right, or was he not standing stock still for a long moment while that Thing glided back and forth, moaning and groaning and rattling its chains — and then was he not creeping slowly *toward* it?

The Perfect Crime was ruined. If Leo had acted like an ordinary, sensible, cowardly human being and streaked for the house, he would have given the master criminals time to remove all incriminating evidence — ghost, chains, clothesline, and all — and get back to the house in time to materialize on the veranda in their pajamas, yawning and asking what was going on.

And when and if the area down by the vegetable garden was investigated with flashlights, not one suspicious thing would have been found. Everyone would have been forced to conclude that Leo had had a nightmare, or a fit of nerves.

But instead there was Leo, creeping slowly forward, until there was nothing for twin fiends to do but drop the ends of the clothesline and scuttle off into the bushes and the brambles, leaving him to discover clipped onto the clothesline an old set of long underwear of Uncle Caleb's, long packed away in a trunk in the attic, with a length of rusty chain tied to the legs.

And Leo, being Leo, did not react to his discovery the way anyone else would have, either. He had proved he really was braver than anyone would have thought possible. All he had to do was carry his captured "ghost" up to the house with a big cocky grin on his face and he would have had the laugh on the twins like nobody's business. He would have made them look so silly they would never have tried to pull anything on him again. In fact, if he had gone about it right, having been so brave and all, he could have made friends with them and had them eating out of his hand all the rest of the summer.

But not Leo. Instead he was white with fury. He stormed and ranted and threw a temper tantrum and was sick in bed all the next day, and neither he nor Aunt Gladys forgave any of us during the rest of their stay. But worst of all was what Dad went through. Because of that remark he had made about "spooks," both Leo and his mother were firmly convinced he knew ahead of time what the twins were planning. Naturally he was outraged by such a suggestion and told everybody off — we got the devil from him, of course, the twins and I — but nothing he could say really convinced Leo and Aunt Gladys. The whole affair was one big family mess.

It took us a while to understand why Leo had been so furious, but finally we did.

His was the fury of *disappointment!*

Leo had thought his wildest hopes were being realized, that he was seeing a real ghost. When it turned out to be a sham it was almost more than he could bear.

If we had not known it before, we knew then that in Cousin Leo our family had a real live oddball.

2

Leo Again

Four

Four years! That made a big difference. Now I was eleven, a year older than Leo had been then. Instead of being a little squirt only seven years of age, I was eleven . . .

But now Leo would be fourteen.

I thought about that and experienced the familiar, hopeless pang felt from time to time by every boy and girl with older brothers and sisters and cousins — that awful feeling of never being able to catch up. By comparison, Leo would still be a big kid and I would be a little kid. Besides which, of course, he would still be Leo, the family's prize pain in the neck.

I had walked forward again to the bow. Now, brooding over the injustice of it all, I turned and flopped down on a bench — and had another kind of familiar experience, one that most of us have at one time or another.

The French call it *déjà vu,* which means "already seen." It is that sudden sensation that what is happening has happened to us before. We know what is coming next even before it happens.

"Hi, sonny!"

I glanced up to find I had sat down next to an old gentleman whose eyes were twinkling at me in a way I had *already seen.* And before he went on, I had that eerie feeling of *déjà vu,* the feeling that I knew exactly what he was going to say next, and what I was going to say in reply. He was going to ask me —

"What's your name?"

"George," I said, "and today's my birthday!"

The words popped out irresistibly, dictated by memory. And now he was going to say —

But then his wife called him, and the sensation was shattered, and vanished.

"Horace! Come here a minute, will you?"

"Oh-oh, there's the boss," he said. "I've got to go. But Happy Birthday anyway, George!"

He walked away, and I stared after him, feeling creepy. Because it wasn't my birthday at all. My birthday came in February, which was when I had met that other old gentleman somewhere years ago, when I was no more than five or six years old. But that was exactly the way our converstation had begun, and in another moment the rest of it would have come back to me. I felt sure it would have. Maybe we would have repeated it, word for word. But no, that didn't make sense, because now it was July, not February, and whatever the first old gentleman said next had had something to do with February. What was it? Where had I been then? Not on a boat, certainly. On a train? On the subway?

It wouldn't' come. It was gone, gone back into the shadowy recesses of that mysterious organ, the human brain.

Was it all some sort of premonition? But how could that be? I knew nothing then about what was waiting on the island. There were no sinister overtones to the incident then; it was just an odd, puzzling experience such as many of us have once in a while. Before I could think any further about it someone spotted a school of fish off our starboard bow and I rushed to the rail to look. One preoccupation led to another, and before long I had forgotten all about the old gentleman.

Well, not quite. Not for good.

One might wonder why, if we felt the way we did about Leo and his mother, we still accepted Aunt Fanny's invitation. Well, Dad *did* talk about how he was darned if he was going out there and put up with those two, but Mom took care of that.

"All right, Paul. If you're going to let them keep you away, if you're going to step aside and let them enjoy a summer of sea air and saltwater swimming while we swelter in the city, I'm sure they will be delighted. Leo's a big boy now, I'm sure he can take care of your share of Aunt Fanny's clam chowders and boiled lobsters —"

Dad groaned.

"— and strawberry shortcakes and blueberry pies and beach plum jelly —"

"Stop! Carol, you're right. I can't let them get away with it. We'll show them! We'll go out there and make *them* miserable!"

I am sure Leo and Aunt Gladys must have thought things over in much the same way and reached similar conclusions. Neither family was about to give up a summer on Broadmoor just because of the other.

One might also wonder why on earth Aunt Fanny would deliberately invite both families to come at the same time. She knew all about the bad blood that had developed over Leo's Ghost. Well, the answer was plain enough if you knew Aunt Fanny. She didn't hold with family feuds. So she was deliberately bringing us together where she could knock some sense into our heads.

The smudge on the horizon broadened, lifted, and took on the contours of an island. The curve of the bluffs ran down to the rocky shoreline, with here and there a small strip of sandy beach gleaming in the sunshine. Soon we could see the jetties that guarded the harbor mouth, and the little town that ringed the small harbor.

The jetties thrust out their welcoming arms, the mailboat pitched and pranced across the choppy water between them, and Dad sang out:

"There's Aunt Fanny in the old blunder-bus!"

All at once he was waving his hat like a schoolboy, unable to hide his excitement any longer, or his emo-

tions. After all, he did have many happy childhood memories of the place, no matter what our last visit had been like, and he was deeply fond of Aunt Fanny.

By now we could all see the old car waiting near the head of the wharf. The mailboat tooted importantly, causing a couple of loungers to amble over to the chocks on the stringpiece at the edge of the wharf, ready to catch lines.

"Good old Broadmoor!" said my father. "There were times when I thought I'd never see it again. I hope —"

"Oh, everything is going to work out fine," said Mom. She was the family optimist.

Aunt Fanny had driven down alone to meet us to save room in the car, since there would be three of us and all our luggage. But I wondered if Leo would have come along even if the car had been twice as large.

"You know, you're all the family I have left, you folks and Gladys and Leo," said Aunt Fanny as she swung the car into Front Street. "I can't tell you how nice it is to have us all together again."

"All the family except the twins, and maybe that's just as well," said Mom.

"Well, yes, maybe that is just as well," agreed Aunt Fanny, and we all had a good cackle.

To my young eyes Aunt Fanny looked the same as ever, old as the hills and yet full of life and still able to take command of any situation the way she always had. She looked as if she were constructed solely of skin and bones, but the strength in her was astounding, the strength and the energy.

In those days women like Aunt Fanny always wore a hat when they went outdoors. She had one on now, a straw affair that looked as if it would have made a good bird's nest. It went well with her old-fashioned dress.

"Wait till you see Leo, you won't know him," she went on, showing she knew exactly what was on our minds. "Shooting up like a weed, thin as a rail —"

"What? Leo thin?"

"That's right, Paul. And he eats enough to keep a shark going, hungry all the time, can't fill him up."

My father listened grimly, and I knew he was congratulating himself on having arrived in time to save at least a few slices of blueberry pie from being wasted on an adolescent's ravenous gullet.

"Still a great reader, though, a great reader — oh, he's a caution! I expect he'll be able to help you a lot with that book you're writing, Paul," Aunt Fanny added with a solemn face that fooled nobody.

"Over my dead body," said Dad with feeling.

"Well, you just be nice to the boy and Gladys and don't make me any trouble, young man," said Aunt Fanny — and it delighted me to hear my father get ordered about and called "young man" — "because everything is going to be forgiven and forgotten, leastways forgiven, and we're all going to get along."

"I'll mind my manners."

"Don't just mind 'em, Paul — *mend* 'em," retorted Aunt Fanny, drawing an enthusiastic "Amen!" from

Mom. "If you think Leo is a scratchy critter, I wish you could have seen yourself at his age."

"*Me?* Why, a gentler, more thoughtful boy has seldom been known to mankind than —"

"Ha! When I think what you were like then, I don't know why I put up with you."

"Aw, come on, Aunt Fanny. I always *was* your favorite!"

"Get on with you! You were — well, more than once when I've watched Leo going through his paces I've thought about you. I don't know but what he takes after you!"

"Aunt Fanny! Watch what you're saying. Even you can go too far!"

In two minutes' time we had left behind all there was of the weatherbeaten, comfortably shabby town and were grinding away up the hill. A clapboarded memory reared up ahead of us and solidified into reality.

"There's the house!" I cried.

"Well, I should hope so," said Aunt Fanny. "A couple of nor'easters tried to blow it out to sea last winter, but it's still there."

The square white frame house with black shutters was amply embellished with the jigsaw curlicues of its period, under the eaves and at the corners, and had a stained-glass window off center at the top of the front stairwell. The house did not look a bit changed, and neither did Aunt Gladys, standing out on the veranda. She had a set, strained smile on her face, as though bracing herself for something unpleasant which she wanted to pretend was pleasant. In all fairness to her, I don't believe she felt all that strongly about us on her own account. She was only worried about her dear Leo and how he felt.

All of us got so busy putting our best foot forward it's surprising there weren't bruised shins all around. Our greetings were sticky with feigned delight. While Aunt Gladys kissed us all effusively, Aunt Fanny looked around and said, "Where's Leo?"

Aunt Gladys's face recaptured some of its strain.

"Why, er, I believe he's out in his tent, reading."

Aunt Fanny's bright old blue eyes glinted as she jerked her head my way.

"Run out and let him know you're here, George, so's he can come say hello to his Aunt Carol and Uncle Paul."

"Yes, ma'm!"

So Leo still had his tent, did he? As I walked around into the backyard I was already planning a campaign for one of my own. I was older now than he had been last time, and *he* had a tent then . . .

What I saw when I turned the corner of the house made me stop and stare long enough to let envy get in a few good nips.

Leo had moved up in the world from pup tent status. He had a real tent now, with a fly held up on two extra poles over the entrance. It was big, plenty big enough for — well, it *would* have been big enough for two if he had been anybody but Leo, I decided bitterly.

I walked to the front and peered in. He was inside,

all right, and he was reading, and he did not look up, even though he knew darn well I was there. For that matter, unless he was deaf he had heard the car come snorting up the gravel driveway. He was being intentionally rude, though I suppose you could hardly blame him for not being anxious to see people who would bring back some of his most humiliating memories.

But even Leo could not ignore a living, breathing presence forever. After a moment he rolled a sullen face up at me, a face that was recognizable but was much longer and thinner than I remembered its being, besides which it now had a few pimples sprinkled over it.

"Oh, it's you," he said, and I almost fell over backward. If he had mooed at me I could not have been more startled.

"Gee! What's the matter, Leo, you got a cold?"

"Certainly not."

"But you sound —"

"Oh." Even though I was standing up looking down at him, Leo managed to look down his nose at me. "My voice changed. Did you think I was going on forever talking in a squeak the way you do?"

I was insulted.

"What do you mean? I don't squeak! I was surprised, that's all. And you used to sound worse, if you want to know!"

Leo received this clumsy thrust with a languid display of contemptuous indifference and went back to his reading while I stood glaring down at him.

"Aunt Fanny said for you to come up and say hello to my folks," I added, glad to have an order to pass along.

He glanced up again and closed his book.

"Those sisters of yours didn't come, did they?"

"No."

"Good."

As he was saying this, and getting more nastiness into a single word than anyone would have thought it could convey, the cover of his book caught my eye — and darned if it didn't have to do with ghosts! *Ghosts of the New England Coast,* it was called.

That was all I needed for a reckless reply.

"It's too bad they're not here, maybe they could show you some more ghosts," I jeered.

Leo pursed his full lips and pushed them out, looking as if he had not heard me. He put his book aside, stood up, and came outside. He was really tall and thin now, and an instant later I learned he was also strong, appallingly strong. Because all at once he grabbed one of my arms and twisted it hard behind my back, so hard my body filled with agonizing flashes of fire.

"Now, listen, you little monkey, that's the last smart crack you're going to make about ghosts, you understand?" he said, and then let me go while I was still gasping from the sudden pain.

"Darn you!" I yelled, and swung at him wildly, but he merely put out one hand and pushed me back so hard I sprawled on my back.

"Shut up. From now on you don't have to talk to me, and I don't have to talk to you."

"Suits me!"

Leo walked away toward the house, leaving me there with my arm still aching and the wind knocked out of me. After a moment of total confusion that featured a feeling of crushing despair, a feeling I had tangled with some sort of ruthless monster who would make my summer one long hell on earth, I scrambled to my feet and followed.

By the time I got there he was dutifully shaking hands with my father and enduring my mother's peck on the cheek. I hated him for his obvious reluctance to accept a kiss from *my mother,* forgetting my similar reaction minutes earlier to his. But at least I had *pretended* better!

Aunt Fanny glanced at my stormy face, checked Leo's, and asked a question.

"What's the matter with you two?"

Leo stiffened, and replied without glancing at me.

"Nothing."

"George?"

"Nothing!"

"Just what kind of 'nothing' do you two mean?"

Leo shrugged.

"We had a difference of opinion. He isn't speaking to me, and that's okay."

"He isn't speaking to me, either, and *that's* okay," I echoed in a shrill voice that came close enough to a squeak to infuriate me.

"Oh? Is that so?"

While the other adults stood around uncomfortably looking everywhere but at each other or at us, Aunt Fanny put her hands on her hips and fixed the two of us with a stare that shriveled even Leo down to size. We felt as if we had been pinned to a board like two insects.

"Well, I'm going to tell you two something right now. It's going to be a long summer, and we're not going to have any feuding, not for a single minute. Now, lunch will be ready in about half an hour, but you won't eat a bite of it till you've made things up between yourselves. The same goes for supper and breakfast tomorrow morning and every other meal till you decide to be friends. And you're not to set foot off the property in the meantime. All right, folks, why don't the rest of us go inside and have some lemonade?"

Five

Aunt Fanny led the way and left two cousins standing there looking foolish. Both Aunt Gladys and my parents were only too glad to hurry inside after her and not have to do anything about us.

Leo and I exchanged baffled glares. But at least he had somewhere to go. He could swing around and march off to his tent and get out of sight. He didn't have to stand around on one foot and then the other, wondering what to do with himself, the way I did. After a moment, feeling very unfairly treated by life, Leo, and Aunt Fanny, I turned and began a slow dawdle around the yard, aimlessly circling the house.

During my first round trip, hands in pockets, scowl on face, feet kicking viciously at any twigs or pebbles foolhardy enough to lie in my path, I was full of defiance and determination. I would starve to death before I would have anything to do with Leo! I'd shown them all!

On my second trip, which featured less kicking and scowling and more thinking, certain unpleasant facts began to occur to me.

First of all, I realized I *was* starving to death.

What with the trip over on the boat through all that invigorating sea air, and the fact that we had eaten breakfast early, and the fact that Mom had not let me buy any candy to eat on the boat, I was empty right down to my shoetops. As long as I had taken it for granted I would be eating before long I had not stopped to think about how hungry I was. Now, faced with the prospect of no lunch, I suddenly could think of nothing but food.

Worse yet, I found myself recalling the reason Mom had not let me buy any candy.

"I don't want you to spoil your appetite, because Aunt Fanny is sure to have something special for lunch, and she's one of the best cooks in New England."

"Offshore or on," agreed Dad. And I could recall just enough about those delightful first two weeks last time, before Leo and Aunt Gladys came and Aunt Fanny went, to know they were not exaggerating.

By the time my third plod around the house took me past the open kitchen windows my condition grew to be truly pitiable. I could not guess exactly what was being cooked in there, but whatever it was produced the most appetizing aroma my poor quivering nostrils had ever inhaled. Much later we learned that Aunt Fanny had set up an electric fan in the kitchen at a strategic angle to make sure the backyard received the full benefit of that aroma.

Both my footsteps and my resolve began to falter. Without admitting to myself that I was ready to negotiate any kind of truce, I decided there would be no harm in drifting past Leo's tent — without so much as glancing his way, you understand — just in case *he* happened to be weakening and was ready to beg my forgiveness in order to get something to eat. I was remembering what Aunt Fanny had said about his appetite. If he ate the way she said he did, then he was poor material for a hunger strike. I figured he must be suffering the tortures of the adolescent damned at the thought of missing a meal.

A casual stroller, glancing this way and that — every way except in the direction of the tent — I sauntered down to have a look at the vegetable garden.

Not a sound came from the tent as I went by. Was he holding his breath and glaring out at me? Apparently he was going to be stubborn. This gave my anger a new lease on life. I marched on down to the vegetable garden telling myself if he could hold out so could I.

Standing there thinking it over I even cast a famished glance at the rows of carrots and turnips, two of my pet hates, and was tempted. For the first time in eleven years they looked edible to me. But something told me Aunt Fanny would somehow know if so much as a single carrot was missing from that garden, even if I got down on my hands and knees and tried to make it appear as if a rabbit had chewed it.

And besides that, Leo would see me!

No, the thing to do, I finally decided, was to ramble back to the yard past the tent again. Going in that direction I would be facing the entrance and would be able to see him out of the corner of my eye without letting him catch me looking his way at all.

So back I went.

The corner of my eye failed to register any Leo lurking inside. Finally, before I was too far past, I was forced to risk a rapid glance straight into the tent, in case he was back in the shadows . . .

But no. Still no Leo! He was not there. He was gone.

Had he disobeyed Aunt Fanny? Had he sneaked away? Excited, I stopped and took a good look inside, half expecting to find the tent cleaned out, with Leo having taken all his belongings and left for good, a rebellious teenager hitting the open road — quite forgetting the fact that on Broadmoor Island the open road did not go very far.

So it was that I was standing there peering into the tent when Leo suddenly appeared, sauntering around a corner of the house.

He stopped and we stared at each other, both caught flatfooted looking for the other. There was no use trying to pretend otherwise. We both knew, and we both knew we both knew.

I will say one thing for Leo, he did not try to pretend. He did not say anything silly like, "What are you doing — looking for me?" He just came over and laid it on the line.

"Okay. Listen. I'm not cutting off my nose to spite my face, not for you or anybody. If you're not hungry after that boat ride —"

"I'm starving!" If he could be honest, so could I, and

I could not have picked a better time to meet him halfway. Leo's small mouth twitched as though it had almost been surprised into a grin, and his heavy frown eased up a little.

"Well, so am I," he admitted. "I could eat a horse."

"I could eat a team of horses!"

Leo let out a snort that had some slight family resemblance to a laugh.

"Okay, then. We'll go in and tell them we're old buddies now. Anything to get some food! We don't have to talk to each other outside — but we've got to make *them* think differently."

"Okay!"

Sweet music interrupted this important conversation. Aunt Fanny had stepped out onto the veranda and was ringing the dinner bell. At the sound of its fine clear tones both of us had to gulp to keep from drooling. Leo turned to me and stuck out his hand.

"Okay, shake," he muttered. "And make it look good."

We shook. After all, when the situation calls for it, when the need is desperate enough, you can always make peace and become allies with someone you detest. Nations do it all the time.

Aunt Fanny glanced our way and looked sternly pleased to see us standing together.

"Okay, Aunt Fanny, we're coming — aren't we, George?"

"Sure, Leo!"

"Well, that's better, boys. Get in here and wash your hands — we're ready to sit down."

Six

It would be impossible to do justice to that meal — the juicy, tender fried pork chops, golden brown and crisply crusted, the mashed potatoes and creamed gravy, the green peas fresh from the garden, and so on — so I won't attempt to describe it. Just take my word for it, Aunt Fanny did give us something to eat.

For quite a while both Leo and I were too busy to take any part in table conversation — not that there was much to take part in at first, anyway; we were not the only ones with good appetites. But after a while, when we had finished and were all sitting back groaning contentedly and talking about how good everything had been, Aunt Fanny brushed aside our compliments and tossed a fateful question at Leo. Fateful, I say, because I have always remembered it as The Beginning.

"Well, Leo, did you read that yarn about Butcher's Cove?"

Aunt Gladys stiffened nervously in her chair and sent an unhappy glance across the round table at Aunt Fanny. She knew what was being referred to, of course, and to her it must have seemed as if a sore spot was being touched on needlessly. Leo's eyes darted around the table, wary and defiant, but then steadied on the old lady as he nodded.

"It's very interesting. Thanks for getting it out for me."

"I'd forgotten all about old Captain Butcher till that piece in last week's paper," said Aunt Fanny, meaning the *Bellport Clarion,* a weekly newspaper put out in the town on the mainland where we had boarded the mailboat.

Dad asked Aunt Fanny the obvious question: "Who was Captain Butcher?"

"Well, he appears to have been a pirate — in fact, there's no doubt about it, the records are clear enough on that score. They hanged him for it! Or did they? No, I recall now, it was — Well, anyway, the important thing about him locally is that he was here a couple of times. And because of an unchristian act he committed the second time he was here — I don't want to spoil the story, you can read it for yourselves — his ghost is supposed to appear over in Butcher's Cove once every hundred years to the day. I guess that'll never make him too much of a tourist attraction, will it?"

"Hardly worth building a grandstand for," agreed

Dad. As always, when listening to Aunt Fanny, he was enjoying himself. "But when did this unchristian act occur?"

"July the eleventh, seventeen hundred and forty-six."

"Ah-ha! And today, if I mistake me not, is July the eighth, nineteen hundred and forty-six. So Captain Butcher's second command performance should be coming up three days from now."

Leo was listening to all of this with a tense, guarded expression, plainly not enjoying my father's satirical attitude. But then —

"Wouldn't be at all surprised," said Aunt Fanny.

She committed herself without a moment's hesitation, and drew a look from Leo I would not have thought him capable of. It was a look of deep and humble gratitude.

"Why, Aunt Fanny," said Dad, surprised, and thrown off stride, "don't tell me you believe in ghosts?"

She took a moment to answer that, calmly marshaling her thoughts as she looked back at him with the eyes of an islander. The minds of those who live their lives on islands surrounded by the sea seldom sink to the prosy depths plumbed by some mainlanders. The atmosphere of their lives won't permit it.

"No," said Aunt Fanny, "I can't say I believe in 'em, but I can't say I disbelieve in 'em, either. I've never seen one, but there's a lot of other things I've never seen, too, things I have to take other folks' word for. I try to keep an open mind.

"It's easy to say a thing is impossible — any fool can do that, and usually does. Yes, indeed, easy to say a thing's impossible, hard to prove it isn't. Nobody has proved for certain there are such things as ghosts — but nobody has proved there aren't, either. So as far as I'm concerned it's an open question and calls for an open mind."

Leo tried to keep up his guard, tried not to lay himself open to the mocking comments he feared, but Aunt Fanny's remarks were too much for him.

"That's the way I feel!" he said passionately. "That's exactly the way I feel!"

Looking back, it amazes me to think how that old lady, for all her seeming forthrightness, could be so subtle. To this day I am not sure that every word she said that day represented her true beliefs, but enough of it was genuine to give her voice the necessary assurance. And fortunately my father was sensitive enough to understand what was going on. He clearly understood what Aunt Fanny had said and why she had said it, and he took his cue from her. He turned to look at Leo with an expression that was completely serious.

"Well, that's fair enough, Leo. There's nothing wrong with investigating *any* question, if you keep an open mind."

Leo could only answer with a nod as he dropped his eyes into a fixed stare down at his empty plate. His nod was so brusque it might have seemed insolent to anyone who did not have some inkling of what was going on inside him, some comprehension of the unexpected, overwhelming satisfaction that was welling up behind his red face. The air was electric, but in that cleansed way that follows a thunderstorm, electric with a feeling of relief, of friction averted, of bygones becoming bygones. There was not going to be any trouble this time about Leo's Ghost. In a sense it had finally been laid to rest, and it was not likely to rise again.

Aunt Fanny picked up the conversation as smoothly as if nothing had happened.

"The fellow that wrote the book I got out for Leo is coming out here Thursday to make a whoop-de-do about Captain Butcher. Name's Marshall Watkins. He's an awful blowhard, but right entertaining — I heard him give a talk once, down at the Hall. Anyway, he's going to Butcher's Cove that night, and I suppose quite a few others will traipse over there with him — enough, probably, so that no self-respecting ghost would think of showing up to be elbowed around by such a crowd, anymore than it did last time, back in eighteen forty-six."

"You mean to say a crowd turned out then?"

"Well, why shouldn't they, Paul? The population in those days was more than it is today, what with the fishing fleet we had then and one thing and another. You can read all about it in the book. Leo, you bring it up to the house for your uncle to see."

At that point I piped up eagerly. Anyone who cannot anticipate my question does not know much about eleven-year-old boys.

"Can we go over to Butcher's Cove that night?"

"Well, we'll see. It's not an easy place to get near to in a car," said Aunt Fanny. "Road pretty well peters out in that direction — swings off toward Crown Head and comes back on that side of the island — but you boys ought to be able to make it all right on the bikes."

Aunt Fanny had the wonderful quality of believing in boys' ability to fend for themselves, one of the many things we learned to love her for. And Leo? Well, by now Leo had recovered himself enough to get back into the conversation, and did so typically — with a complaint.

"I hope the weather's bad, so all the curiosity-seekers won't come and spoil everything — and that includes Marshall Watkins," he groused, looking like one of those moody busts of Beethoven so beloved by music teachers. "I'll bet he *is* an awful blowhard, like Aunt Fanny says. He'll try to turn the whole thing into a publicity stunt."

It was obvious that Leo wished he could have the whole place out there all to himself. Well, he couldn't keep *me* away if I wanted to go, because now Aunt Fanny had reminded me of the existence of two bicycles out in the barn, and he could not very well ride both of them. I knew they were there because he and the twins had been squabbling about them all the time four years ago.

I wondered how far it was to Butcher's Cove.

As soon as we were excused from the table I slipped outside and made a beeline to the barn to see the bikes.

I would find out which one Leo used, the red one or the blue one — I didn't want any trouble on that score — and the other one would be mine.

Inside the barn it was cool and almost dark, with a pleasantly musty smell as if a few bundles of hay might still be up in the loft somewhere. As I walked around on the rattly plank floor, looking things over, I was astonished to see hanging from a nail the very length of chain the girls had used for Leo's Ghost. It had probably been hanging right there from that day to this, from the time Dad, thundering like some Old Testament prophet, had made the twins put it back where they found it. I don't know why things like that seem so surprising, but they always do.

I drifted back toward the house. Leo was crossing the yard toward his tent. It annoyed me to find myself caught in the act of coming out of the barn. Why do we always feel another person is immediately going to guess what we have been up to? I was sure he had seen me come out. He didn't pay any attention to me, however, but just kept on going and disappeared into his tent.

Once again I was at loose ends. I felt like doing something, like having some fun, but what was there to do? I thought about the baseball and glove I had brought along and wished Leo had been a different kind of kid, one who did normal things like playing catch and who might have been willing to play catch with me. Fat chance! He wouldn't even know how to catch a ball.

On the other hand, there was Dad. If only I could get him to come out and throw a few, that would show Leo something! He might even be jealous and wish he *did* know how to play.

I went into the house and looked around hopefully for my father. I found him arranging his papers and books in the back room upstairs that was to be his study, the same room the twins had been in when they were with us.

"Hey, Dad, will you play catch with me?"

He gave me a preoccupied look in the midst of taking his portable typewriter out of its case.

"Later, son, later. I want to get myself set up here before I do anything else."

"Okay, I'll get the ball and gloves and be outside."

"Later."

"You said you were going to get plenty of exercise," I reminded him. You have to keep after fathers when you are trying to get them to play catch with you.

"Okay, okay, I will — later! Now beat it!"

His tone of voice was discouraging. I found the bag with the ball and gloves in it and took them outside, but I knew the prospects were none too good. Dad would be fooling around in there for a long time. Sighing, feeling sorry for myself, I began to toss up some pop flies.

The trouble with that, of course, is that it is very hard to throw straight up. I grunted three or four pretty fair tosses into the air, and only dropped one of them, but then my next throw went wild.

It arced across the yard in a trajectory that seemed certain to bring it down smack on top of Leo's tent — and wouldn't I hear about that! But it faded just enough to bounce off a tent peg and roll down the slope toward the vegetable garden, stopping just as Leo came charging outside.

He looked down at the baseball as if he had never seen one before and didn't like what he saw now. Then he looked at me. Even though we were not supposed to be speaking outside the house, it was difficult not to do so now if he wanted to find out what was going on.

"What do you think you're doing?"

"I was throwing up pop flies and one got away from me."

He looked at the ball again. Then he picked it up, turned — and whipped it back to me with the sweetest motion you ever saw.

I caught it and stood goggling at him as he turned and went back into his tent.

Now I was really annoyed. An arm like that wasted on Leo, a guy who wouldn't have anything to do with anybody! But then, before I could get my resentment into really high gear, he was back again — and lo and behold, he had a fielder's glove on his hand!

"Gosh! Do you play ball?"

"Who's there to play ball with out here?" he snapped. "Sure I play. I play ball at school. I have to, because I'm good," he added gloomily.

"What do you play?"

"Center field. Everybody has to play something, and

baseball isn't as stupid as most games, so that's what I play. And anyway, even though I don't like to waste my time on athletics, I believe in getting exercise and keeping fit. Out here I sometimes bounce a tennis ball against the barn doors just for exercise," he muttered, as though mentioning a secret and shameful vice.

I threw the ball back to him in a tentative, experimental way, and he sighed, but it worked. We played catch for a long time without saying another word. It was hard to tell whether Leo was enjoying it or not, but I certainly was.

After a while he brought our game to an abrupt end.

"Okay, that's enough," he said, and gave the ball a final toss back to me. "Come here a minute," he ordered, and plunged into his tent in that hurried, impatient way that was characteristic of him. By the time I got there he had come out with a book in his hand.

"Here, take this to your father."

"Okay."

It was the book he had been reading the first time I had seen him in his tent: *Ghosts of the New England Coast*, by Marshall Watkins. He seemed ready to dive out of sight again, but then turned back almost grudgingly for a last word.

"The part about Butcher is Chapter Four," he snapped. "You can read it if you want to."

I was ridiculously pleased, and had to bite my tongue not to thank him.

"Okay, I will!"

He was already gone. I turned away and looked

around eagerly for a nice grassy spot under a tree.

Chapter Four in Marshall Watkins's book bore the lurid title "Butchery in Butcher's Cove." A promising beginning. Sitting in the shade of a tall sycamore tree, with my back against the smooth trunk, this is what I read:

3

Captain Butcher

Ghosts of the
New England Coast

$\mathcal{S}$o far we have stayed along the coast of New England, but this next yarn will take us a few miles *off* the coast, out to picturesque, salt-sprayed Broadmoor Island. And although it is more of a murder story than a pirate story, and more of a pirate story than a ghost story, it is well worth the trip, being a tale well calculated to shiver our timbers!

Broadmoor Island is about eight miles long and five miles wide. The only town, nestled around the little harbor on the southwest side of the island, is Newgate. Whoever provided those place names must have been some gallows bird with a ghoulish sense of humor, because Newgate was a famous prison back in London, and Broadmoor was an asylum for the criminally insane!

Indeed, it is said that the island's first settlers were a motley crew who needed to put a little comfortable distance between themselves and the forces of the law, but then that's another story! At any rate, sometime in the very early 1700s a settlement was begun.

Even then, beyond the harbor village that was Newgate most of the island remained uninhabited, with its long stretches of grim and rockbound shoreline, with here and there a small strip of sandy beach where a pirate captain could slip ashore and bury treasure if he wanted to.

That is just what one of them did one dark and moonless night in the year of Our Lord seventeen hundred and forty-five.

But now, before we get to that night, we have to leave chilly New England and travel south to the torrid climes of the Caribbean Sea, from whence Spanish galleons were rolling across the Spanish Main homeward bound to Cadiz and Malaga and Barcelona laden with the riches of the West Indies and South America.

England and Spain were at war, as usual. This made enemy ships fair game for anyone able to capture them. Privateers were everywhere, and privateering was often as not no more than a polite name for piracy. Indeed, the Caribbean spawned the greatest age of piracy in the history of the world, an age which at the time of our story had only recently begun its long decline.

Living ashore in Kingston, capital of the island of Jamaica, was a discontented officer of the British navy, Lieutenant Randall. He was recovering from wounds received at the attack by a British fleet on the ports of La Guayra and Porto Cavallo on the South American coast.

Although Randall had a brilliant reputation as a shiphandler, he had been passed over when his promotion to captain might have been possible because Commodore Knowles could not bring himself to trust Randall. How correct Knowles's judgment was may be judged by later events! Even in those hard-bitten times Randall seemed unusually ruthless and unscrupulous.

When he had recovered from his wounds he did not present himself to return to duty. Instead he fell in with a group planning a privateering expedition, became captain of their ship, the *Speedwell*, and made an extremely profitable voyage, capturing three prizes.

The principal backer of the expedition was a wealthy sugar planter named Tyndall, who had started his own career in questionable ways at sea. He had not been unknown in the pirate republic of New Providence, on the island where Nassau now flourishes peaceably as a tourist resort.

Randall had become friendly with Andrew Tyndall and his brother Henry. During their drinking bouts together Andrew had often fallen to boasting about a hoard of priceless jewels he had taken from a cathedral during the sacking of a Spanish colonial city many years earlier. From what Tyndall said, it became clear to Randall that the planter still had the jewels in his possession. Bit by bit, and with such patience as never to arouse Andrew's suspicions, Randall gradually formed a very good idea as to where the jewels were hidden.

Randall's second-in-command on *Speedwell* was a red-bearded young renegade named Jabez Tompkins. The two had recognized each other as birds of a feather and become close friends. Randall now drew Tompkins into a scheme he had in mind.

A second voyage for *Speedwell* was planned, and all was in readiness. The night before the ship was to sail,

Randall and Tompkins were among a group drinking together in a waterfront tavern, a group that included the Tyndall brothers.

Slipping away during the height of the festivities, Randall and Tompkins rode pell-mell to the Tyndall plantation. Two sleepy slaves, house servants who were unlucky enough to appear when the men arrived, had their throats cut before they could even cry out. Then, while Tompkins stood guard, Randall checked out his theory about the hiding place of the jewels and found it was spectacularly correct.

He had no more than placed his loot in a bag when he heard cries outside and the clash of steel on steel. The Tyndall brothers had returned unexpectedly and were attacking the intruder they had discovered!

Drawing a pistol from his belt, Randall walked outside and calmly shot Andrew Tyndall through the heart. Henry was so surprised he dropped his cutlass. At that instant Tompkins lunged forward and ran him through. Henry's body fell across that of his brother.

The two villains were now joined in a more serious bond than they had planned. Robbery was one thing, but the murder of two prominent citizens was another. They knew their best chance now lay in putting to sea before the bodies were found and the alarm was spread.

They returned to the ship, rounded up the crew, and gave orders to sail.

And now a veil of secrecy falls over the movements of *Speedwell*. Certain it must be that Randall declared for out-and-out piracy and no return to Jamaica, and had little trouble persuading the crew to this course, which meant much larger shares of the loot for all. At any rate, once she had put a safe distance between him and Jamaica, Randall laid her to in the lee of some uninhabited island where, under his shrewd guidance, the crew sharpened her up into an even smarter sailer than before.

Apparently Randall had many revolutionary and farsighted ideas along this line, which the stodgy English admirals had been unwilling to listen to, and this was one of the reasons he turned against the service. If he had been an honest officer of His Majesty's Navy, willing to work patiently to get his ideas accepted, Randall might have won his name a creditable place in naval history, but this was not to be. Instead of making a place for his name in history, he discarded it entirely. From that time forward he began to make infamous the name of Captain Butcher.

His choice of a name shows a grim sense of humor, though it is likely he chose the name in order to strike additional terror into the hearts of all who might run afoul of his black ship, with its skull-and-crossbones fluttering from a masthead.

Working north through the Florida Straits, *Speedwell* took several ships, making no nice distinctions between enemy and friendly merchantmen, and selling captured cargoes at certain places along the southern coast of the American colonies where no questions were asked so long as profits were large.

It was evident, however, that the great days of piracy were passing. The trade was becoming unsafe. Twice *Speedwell* ran afoul of British men-of-war and barely escaped being blasted out of the water. Butcher followed the Gulf Stream farther north, a thoughtful man.

News traveled slowly in those days, but there was still the danger that his and Tompkins's crimes would become known wherever they went, making them marked men.

Captain Butcher decided to let his beard grow.

Unlike the more famous pirate Blackbeard, he had always remained clean-shaven at sea, both during his service in His Majesty's Navy and his privateering days. He told his crew he was growing a beard for luck, but actually it was part of a plan which was forming in the diabolical captain's mind.

Perhaps Butcher was beginning to weary of a life of bloodshed and debauchery. Certainly he was beginning to think it might be pleasant to leave the sea and go ashore somewhere to live like a gentleman on his ill-gotten gains — under a new assumed name, of course!

Furthermore, Butcher had a secret he longed to be free of. Although he had pretended to share the Tyndall jewels equally with Tompkins, actually he had held back the most priceless part of the collection, a necklace of enormous value. It got so he could hardly sleep for fear Tompkins or any one of his rascally crew might somehow come to know of it.

He determined to do something that few if any other pirates had ever done. He decided to bury his treasure.

Most pirates spent their share of prize money as fast as they got it, never gathered together much treasure, and certainly never buried any of it. Actual instances of ordinary pirates burying treasure are almost unheard of. But Butcher was no ordinary pirate, and, for that matter, his great treasure had not come to him through piracy.

One placid summer night, having sailed far north to evade pursuit by a dogged naval squadron, *Speedwell* found anchorage in a small cove on an island which captured charts told Butcher was Broadmoor Island. Here he saw the opportunity he wanted.

A bowl of rum punch was mixed for the usual drinking bout, and soon the crew was drunk to the last man and fast asleep — except for the captain and his second-in-command.

A dinghy was already in the water alongside, since men had been sent ashore earlier to look for fresh water. Butcher told Tompkins he wanted to go ashore alone, and told him it would be well worth his while to keep watch while he was gone and see to it the crew had no reason to notice their captain's absence. Tompkins readily agreed.

Butcher carefully lowered a canvas-wrapped bundle into the boat, and — as Tompkins well knew — there were a couple of spades in her which the men had left there. That he put two and two together and was astonished by the answer he got seems most likely, but he was too prudent to ask questions.

After a few final whispered words about keeping a good watch, Captain Butcher went hand over hand down a line into the boat, unshipped the oars, and rowed quietly away toward land, disappearing into the darkness of a moonless night.

Two or three hours later he returned, silently handed a handsome jeweled ring to his "friend" Tompkins, and that was that. Again Tompkins was smart enough to ask no questions of Butcher, though he well may have been asking a good many of himself.

But now Butcher took Tompkins into his confidence on another matter, and here he spoke more freely. He told him frankly he thought there was no future for them in staying with the ship. In the old days they could have done what thousands of pirates did — surrender themselves and their ships to the British authorities and receive pardons from His Gracious Majesty. Even now, perhaps, the crew could have done that — but how about themselves? For them there would be no pardon, but rather a trip to the gallows — for murder.

On the other hand, if it was thought that they had been lost at sea, they could then settle somewhere ashore and begin a comfortable new life, living off the proceeds of the Tyndall booty . . .

Tompkins found himself in complete agreement with this line of thinking. Together they hatched a devilish plot.

Sometime earlier *Speedwell* had taken a valuable cargo of cloth from a Bristol ship bound for Charleston. Butcher now gave out a story to the crew of knowing about certain merchants in a nearby Massachusetts coastal town who could be counted on to take the cargo off their hands at a good price. Slipping toward shore at nightfall, they found good anchorage near the mouth of a secluded cove a few miles from the nearest settlement.

"And Jabez," said Captain Butcher, stroking his new black beard, "I want you to go shave off those ruddy whiskers of yours! Two fine beards on this vessel is one too many!"

The men guffawed at this rough joke, while Tompkins went grumbling away to obey the captain's orders. Actually, this was also part of the plan. Tompkins had always worn a beard, Butcher never had; the change in their appearance would help to disguise them in case they should ever cross the tracks of some old tar or naval officer who had known them in the service or in Jamaica. Such was the wiliness and ability to plot of Captain Butcher!

Leaving the crew to their evening drinking bout, Butcher and Tompkins went ashore, ostensibly to make arrangements.

While the two villains slipped over the side and rowed hard for the mainland, however, slow fuses were burning deep in one of *Speedwell's* holds, uncomfortably close to the powder kegs. Not long after they had reached shore there was a tremendous explosion out to sea. *Speedwell* settled into the water with all hands lost.

*T*he explosion was heard in the nearest settlement — exactly as Butcher had planned it — and the next morning at low tide the inhabitants flocked out in small boats to the wreck, which was then clearly visible above water.

Some water-soaked documents were found on the beach at the high waterline, having apparently floated ashore — actually, Butcher and Tompkins had planted them there — and from these documents the ship's identity was learned. Word of the wreck was sent to the British admiralty, and it was assumed that Captain Butcher and his pirate crew were no more, and good riddance.

By that time a Mr. Cuthbert and a Mr. Bothwell had appeared in Boston, established themselves in a pleasant red brick house, and begun living the life of gentlemen.

For about a year the two villains seemed to live together on excellent terms, but you may be sure that neither of them forgot for one minute about Butcher's mysterious errand ashore on Broadmoor Island. They must have played a cat-and-mouse game the entire time, with Butcher sitting back patiently, making no move to revisit the island, and Tompkins waiting just as patiently, ever on the alert to see what Butcher would do.

There was also an incident in which both men became interested in obtaining the favors of the same lady. By this time, living a life of ease ashore, Captain Butcher was already becoming heavy-set, and besides that, his large black beard did not add to his charms from the lady's standpoint. Since Tompkins was not only clean-shaven but younger and handsomer anyway, it is not surprising the lady preferred him to the dark, paunchy Butcher.

Butcher pretended to take lightly his defeat in the court of Venus, but secretly he began to hate Tompkins, and he plotted his revenge from that moment on.

In the spring of 1746, then, Butcher began to talk about taking a little trip out to an island to get a whiff of sea air, always accompanying these remarks to Tompkins with sly winks and grins. Tompkins, of course, showed interest, but did his best not to seem too excited.

Presently, having dangled his bait above the water, Butcher dropped it in.

"Why don't you come with me?" he asked Tompkins. "I'd be glad of the company, besides which two strangers aren't as conspicuous as one. A single stranger always rouses more suspicions."

Tompkins agreed that this was a very sagacious way of looking at things, whereupon Butcher pressed him even more persuasively. Acting as though he were letting bygones be bygones and allowing his old fondness for his shipmate to come to the fore, he clapped him on the shoulder and permitted himself to use Tompkins's real name.

"Jabez, you're a good lad, and my one friend in all the world. If you'll come with me, I may let you in for a share of something very pretty. Very pretty indeed!"

Tompkins said he thought the offer sounded attractive, and without further ado Butcher began arranging ways and means to get to Broadmoor Island.

First they spent several days going by stagecoach to Bellport, then as now the mainland town closest to the island. There Butcher arranged with the owner of a fishing smack to take them out to the island, wait for them a day or two if necessary, and bring them back. The money he offered was more than enough to satisfy the simple fisherman.

Now, one thing our two scoundrels could not disguise about themselves was their former occupation — as men of the sea, that is. The rolling gait of a seaman and a dozen other telltale characteristics were enough to give them away to anyone who lived by the sea, and they knew it. So they passed themselves off as ex–naval officers who had been given the semi-official errand of checking certain topographical features of the island which were hard to observe accurately from the sea but should be shown on the charts.

When they reached Broadmoor they of course gave out the same story there, and such was the persuasiveness of Captain Butcher that the story was accepted lock, stock, and barrel.

It was by then almost evening. They found a house along the waterfront where they could engage a couple of rooms for their stay — there were no inns in the tiny settlement then, to be sure, and only one small shop that had a bit of everything for sale, including grog and ale, as Captain Butcher did not fail to notice on the way past.

As soon as the two men were alone Butcher became very communicative. He drew up a chair to a rough table, urged Tompkins to do the same, and spread a piece of paper flat on the table. It was a hand-drawn map. With his seaman's eye Tompkins knew it at once to be a portion of the shore of the island, since at the time of their former visit he had carefully noted certain features, including two stone towers, which were drawn on the map.

As it happens, a visionary but not very practical official of the British navy had already shown interest in Broadmoor Island some years earlier. Dangerous shoals lay offshore near the cove where *Speedwell* had once anchored. The official, Sir Alfred Busby, caused two stone towers to be erected on Broadmoor — called East Light and West Light to this day — on which fires were to be tended in all periods of bad weather in order to warn ships off the shoals.

Unfortunately Sir Alfred failed to arrange for adequate maintenance of these beacons, with the result that they were soon neglected and eventually abandoned altogether. By the time *Speedwell* paid her fateful visit to the island they were no longer tended, but West Light was a prominent landmark on the bluff behind the cove.

"Now, this area is where I want to go to make my 'observations,' " said Captain Butcher, with more sly winks. "I'd calculate it to be not more than three miles from here across the southern side of the island. But I gather low tide won't be till after dark, and I need a good low tide for my activities, so I don't see much point in stumbling around in the dark when we can just as well take a ramble in broad daylight, when the tide's low again in the morning. There won't be a living soul around out there to see us, anyway. What do you say?"

Tompkins declared himself all in favor of waiting for daylight. Butcher then yawned mightily and said, "Well, this has been thirsty work. Didn't I spy a place a few doors back that might have some ale in it? See if there isn't a boy downstairs can fetch us some."

Tompkins went off willingly on this errand and was gone for some time. When he returned he was carrying two foaming tankards in one hand and a pitcher of ale in the other.

"I couldn't find a boy, so I fetched it myself," he explained, and set a tankard before Captain Butcher. They clanked tankards together in a genial toast and drained them in a single draught.

"There, that's more like it," said Butcher, licking his lips and wiping ale off his dark, bushy beard. He watched with sleepy satisfaction while Tompkins re-filled his tankard from the pitcher. "Another mug of this and I'll be ready for a good nap before supper. I'm fagged out. I wonder, though, if you shouldn't go look out our boatman and tell him to stand by for midday on the morrow?"

"I'll do that," agreed Tompkins.

"And another thing, ask someone for the loan of a spade," said Butcher, with more of his winks and grins. "Tell them we're going to take samples of the soil, and maybe dig a few clams for the fun of it."

This time Tompkins grinned back at him.

"I'll do that, too," he promised.

Butcher's mouth gaped in another cavernous yawn, and he stumbled to his feet.

"Well, it's forty winks for me. Don't know when I've been so bone weary," he mumbled, looking down at the table with bleary eyes. He picked up the map with clumsy fingers and fumbled with it, trying to stuff it into his pocket as he weaved toward the bed, but it fell to the floor instead, and Butcher collapsed onto the bed with something between a grunt, a groan, and a snore.

Tompkins sat watching the motionless figure for a long time. Then with a low chuckle he rose, picked up the map, and left the room, shutting the door quietly behind him.

$\mathscr{W}$hen it came to a game of wits, however, Tompkins was no match for the wily Butcher. One night at an inn during their journey from Boston to Bellport, when Tompkins had drunk a good deal and gone to sleep first, Butcher had searched his clothes and found in one pocket exactly what he had expected to find: a vial of white powder.

He knew from long experience that it was a powder which, when added to a drink, would send a man to sleep for at least twenty-four hours. He had expected this and was prepared for it. Emptying the small vial, he substituted a harmless white powder he had brought with him, then returned the vial to its place in Tompkins's pocket.

So now, as soon as he heard Tompkins leave the house, Butcher rose and went slowly downstairs, acting very sleepy. The old woman they had rented their rooms from looked at him in surprise.

"Why, sir, I thought you was a-sleeping," she said. "The other gentleman said you was, and not to disturb you even if you slept till morning or after."

"I tried to sleep, but I don't feel well," said Butcher. "When he comes back, tell him I've gone out for a stroll to clear my head and will return shortly."

He said that merely as a precaution, for he was pretty certain Tompkins would not be returning to the house. Tompkins would be looking for the fisherman to tell him to be ready to sail before midnight, and then Tompkins would be finding someone who would lend him a spade.

And the doing of those errands would take up enough time to give Butcher a good head start for the cove!

The only part of the escapade Butcher did not enjoy was the three-mile walk. Seamen are seldom fond of walking. But there was no other way to get there inconspicuously, so he stumped along as fast as he could.

It was already near on to dusk when he set out. At first he kept to low places wherever he could, to avoid being seen at a distance, but before long it grew dark enough so that he no longer had to worry. In an hour's time he had reached the stone tower that stood near the cove.

He climbed to the top of the twenty-foot tower, which stands to this very day, and there, crouched down behind the ramparts, he mounted watch on the moors that lay between him and the village. Perhaps the name Broadmoor was not altogether a joke, because the rolling expanses of the island do resemble the wild moors of Scotland.

Behind him down on the little beach, stones rattled on the sand as the tide slowly ebbed. Butcher watched and waited, sure of his prey. And presently he saw a dim spot of light moving across the moors toward him. It was Tompkins. He was carrying a spade on his shoulder and a dark lantern in his hand which threw a circle of light around his hurrying feet.

As soon as he saw Tompkins coming Butcher left the tower, slipped over the side of the low bluff, and descended to the beach, where he found a large boulder off to one side to hide behind.

Before long he heard the scrabble of Tompkins's footsteps on the bluff above him. Down came Tompkins, slipping and sliding in his eagerness. Laying aside his spade he consulted the map by the light of his lantern, which shone clearly on his greedy face. Then he began to get his bearings and to pace off distances with great care. When he had marked off the right line to his satisfaction he took up the spade, set the lantern nearby, and began to dig.

For a long time Fortune did not smile on his efforts. The hole he was digging widened and deepened. It was hard work; he grunted and groaned, but greed kept him feverishly at his labors. Then, at last! — his spade struck something! Tompkins went to his hands and knees and dug wildly with his fingers as rotted cloth came away in shreds by the handful. Finally, with a glad cry, he lifted a small box — a jewel casket! — out of the hole!

The scrape of a footstep behind him made him whirl around. There stood a dark figure pointing a pistol at his head. An evil chuckle chilled his heart, fire flashed from the muzzle, and Jabez Tompkins, his prize already tumbling aside from his nerveless fingers, fell forward — into the grave he had dug for himself!

"Thankee, Jabez, for saving me all that work," said Butcher with a savage guffaw. Prizing open the jewel box with his knife, Butcher thrust its priceless contents into his pocket, then tossed the box down beside the lifeless body.

"Here's your casket, Jabez," he snarled, and laughed again as he picked up the spade and began to fill in the grave.

When Butcher returned to the village and walked to the wharf he found the boat ready and waiting, as he had expected.

"Are we to go, sir?" asked the fisherman.

"Yes, but the other gentleman is going to stay out here while I go ashore for some additional equipment we need," said Butcher. "I'll be a few days ashore, and I'll pay you well for another trip when I return."

Happy with his windfalls and the prospect of more, the fisherman set off, and they were soon on a broad reach for the mainland. Butcher could feel confident there would be no hue and cry over Tompkins's disappearance. The fisherman would wait and wonder and scratch his head for a while, but no one would bother to search the whole island for a missing stranger no one cared about.

Butcher's revenge was complete.

*B*ut now we must turn back the clock again a year or so to the night *Speedwell* met her terrible end.

In the town of Barnham lived a retired British naval captain named Wycroft. Barnham was no great distance from the scene of the wreck, but as luck would have it Wycroft was closer still to the scene that night, as he happened to be visiting a friend in the village nearest the location of the wreck.

Being of a curious turn of mind, especially concerning affairs of the sea, Wycroft was early upon the scene after the disaster became known. The gray light of daybreak had barely begun to make any sort of investigation possible before Wycroft had joined the others who made their way to the site.

Now, Captain Wycroft was the sort of man who, a century or so later, would have made a good candidate for Scotland Yard. He noticed many things that other persons did not notice.

For example, he was present when the water-soaked documents were found on the beach. The men who found them were interested only in the fact that the documents made it possible to identify the vessel. Captain Wycroft, however, thought to himself that it was odd so many documents had washed ashore so close to one another instead of having been scattered this way and that along the beach.

When a stove-in dinghy was found in shallow water a bit farther along, others simply assumed it to be part of the wreckage that had washed ashore. Wycroft waded out to give it a closer inspection, and could not convince himself the holes in it were the product of any explosion.

Unfortunately his exertions that morning caused Captain Wycroft to catch a chill, which confined him to his bed for the next few days. But as he lay there, he brooded. By now the vessel had been definitely identified as *Speedwell,* lately a pirate ship under the command of the notorious Captain Butcher, so that now Wycroft's suspicions doubled.

The fact that *Speedwell* had come to grief was not in itself a source of suspicion. Pirates were their own worst enemies. Pirate ships were frequently wrecked because of the carelessness and lack of discipline that was characteristic of their crews. But in this case, brooded Wycroft, why had a pirate vessel anchored conveniently near the shore and then blown up, sending all on board to certain death? Why were identifying documents found conveniently strewn along the beach, all within a few yards of one another? And what about that dinghy? Was it really part of the wreckage or had it been holed *after* someone had come ashore in it?

After a couple of days of this Wycroft was cursing his illness and impatient to get back on his feet, because there were things he wanted to do. Being a gentleman of leisure and possessed of a modest fortune left him by an uncle in England, he was able to pursue whatever investigations he chose to — and pursue them he did! Against the advice of his physician Wycroft got himself out of bed, had a favorite mare saddled, and rode off on a round of those neighboring villages which were closest to the scene of the wreck.

Wycroft had taken up the scent!

Everywhere he asked the same questions. Had any strangers appeared in town on the previous Wednesday or Thursday, or at any time since?

At first his inquiries were fruitless, but in the third town he tried he struck home. Yes, on Thursday two strangers, well-dressed gentlemen, one heavily bearded and the other clean-shaven, had appeared in town saying they had walked over from a smaller village where they were visiting and that they wished to hire horses in order to ride to the shore and view the wreck about which word had just been brought to them.

They offered handsome terms, with the result that horses were quickly procured. Yes, they had looked as if they might well be men who had been to sea. As was so often the case with seafaring men, neither cut a good figure on horseback or seemed at ease in the saddle.

The two men had not returned, however. Instead, the horses had been sent back two days later — only the day before Wycroft was making his inquiries — from a larger town a few miles down the coast . . .

Wycroft's own town!

According to the lad who brought them back, the two gentlemen had appeared with heavy bags strapped behind them on their horses and had made it well worth the lad's while to return the horses for them. No, the lad had not known what they did or where they went after that — Knyvet Dawkins's boy, he had been, and not the brightest one who ever came down the pike. He did recall, however, after considerable head-scratching, that the gentlemen had inquired about stagecoaches.

Wycroft speculated on their movements. Where had they gone after hiring the horses? Was it not probable that they had ridden in the direction of the wreck to some secluded spot near the shore, some spot where they had cached whatever it was they had brought with them from the ship? And having retrieved this "luggage," had they not then ridden down the coast until they came to the larger town of Barnham?

Wycroft hurried home as fast as his stout mare could carry him and went straight to the stagecoach inn. There he learned that the two strangers, well burdened with luggage, had taken the stagecoach going south two days earlier.

Hastily collecting together what articles he needed for the journey, Wycroft set off on horseback, determined to overtake the stagecoach and learn the identity of the two men — and perhaps find out what they had been carrying in that heavy luggage of theirs!

Once again, however, fickle Fortune failed to favor the dogged Wycroft.

A violent rainstorm slowed his pace to a plod for many hours. When he finally reached Ipswich, saddle-sore, chilled to the bone, and feverish again, it was only to learn that the stagecoach had come and gone. Worse yet, the two passengers he was pursuing had left the coach there, purchased a pair of hacks from a livery stable without haggling over the outrageous price asked for them, strapped their belongings onto the sturdy mounts, and ridden away — no one knew where!

Not only had Captain Wycroft lost the scent, he had reached the limits of his endurance as well. Giddy with fever, he was put to bed in the inn, and for several days he was desperately ill.

When at last he was fit to travel there seemed nothing to do but return home, admitting defeat. He told the landlord of the inn to send word to him if ever he saw the two men again. He had done the same thing everywhere along the road at each stopping point on the stagecoach route, giving assurance of a handsome reward for information. Beyond that there seemed little more Captain Wycroft could do to further the cause of justice.

Justice, yes — for by now he was firmly convinced that the two men had come from *Speedwell* and were probably her notorious captain and some accomplice.

Several months had passed when personal business

took Captain Wycroft to Boston, where he chanced to meet an old naval acquaintance also retired, one Captain Fielding.

Captain Fielding, though a fine officer with a meritorious career at sea to his credit, was in no way as comfortably fixed as Captain Wycroft, besides which he had recently suffered severe financial losses through an ill-advised speculation. When Wycroft chanced to meet him, Fielding was hoping to scrape a passage back to England, where Heaven knows what penurious existence awaited him.

The two captains, however, soon found one another to be the best of companions, with the result that Wycroft warmly urged Fielding to return to Barnham with him for an extended visit. He described his existence there in such attractive terms — and, indeed, it was a most comfortable existence — that Captain Fielding would have been strange indeed had he resisted the invitation. They set off for Barnham together.

$\mathcal{D}$uring the homeward journey the subject of the wreck of the *Speedwell* came up — in fact, it was Fielding who brought it up.

"I say, Wycroft, wasn't *Speedwell* lost somewhere near you?" he asked as they rattled along in the stage-coach.

"Quite near," said Wycroft.

"Bad business, that rascal Randall and all," said Fielding. "I was with Knowles, in command of *Perseverance,* when Randall was one of his lieutenants on *Strafford.* Let's see, that would have been back in —"

"Did you know Randall?" cried Wycroft eagerly. By then he had long since learned the whole story of *Speedwell* and her villainous officers, including the murders of the Tyndall brothers in Jamaica.

"Aye, knew him well, the blackhearted devil, and never trusted him, even then!" replied Fielding. "Nor did the commodore, for that matter. But to think he would turn himself into a sea-devil with a name like Butcher! Came to a well-deserved end, if you were to ask me."

"*If* he did meet that end," murmured Wycroft in a tone that immediately caught his friend's attention. Delighted to have so suitable an audience, Wycroft poured out the whole story of his suspicions and his pursuit of the two strangers. And certainly he could not have found a more receptive listener than Captain Fielding.

"Damn me, if Randall *did* blow up his own ship and slip away alive, I'd like to see him laid by the heels for it!" growled Fielding.

"And so would I," said Wycroft, strangely excited, "and I feel it in my bones that we shall! I tell you, I feel it in my bones! I have men at a dozen inns along this very road between Boston and Barnham on the lookout for that pair — and now I have you, a man who can identify Butcher if ever we pick up his trail again! Providence works in wondrous ways, and I sincerely believe that Providence brought us together for a purpose!"

At the first opportunity, once they were home in Barnham, Wycroft took his friend to the scene of the disaster — the bones of the wreck were still visible at low tide — and together they went over the ground carefully, weighing and considering everything.

Now, a visit in those days was nothing like today's visits, when a month is usually considered a long stay. Visits of three to six months or even a year were not uncommon, especially when the host was genuinely anxious to have his guest prolong his stay. Actually, after a month or two, Wycroft wanted nothing more than to enjoy Fielding's company indefinitely. Whenever Fielding said anything about feeling he should be moving on, Wycroft reminded him of the pirate

Butcher and urged him to wait a bit longer, just in case some word of the villain should reach them. "Waiting for Butcher" became a little joke between them, and time passed pleasantly . . .

And then word came!

Early on the morning of July 11, 1746, the two retired captains returned from an overnight stay in a neighboring town to learn that the innkeeper at the local stagecoach stop had been urgently inquiring for Captain Wycroft. Setting off for the inn at a gallop, they found exciting news awaiting them.

Two men had come through on the stage the previous evening and the innkeeper was certain they were the men Captain Wycroft had been looking for!

Wycroft cursed the way in which Fortune had once again played him false. If only he and Fielding had been at home when the stage arrived Butcher and his accomplice might even now be in the hands of the authorities! Still, Fortune had not been completely cruel: the innkeeper had heard the pair making inquiries about the road to Bellport.

Pausing only to change horses, the captains took up the trail. At each stage along the way they checked to make sure their quarry had not alighted. It was late afternoon when finally they reached Bellport. There they heard what they had been hoping for: two men who fitted the descriptions had left the stagecoach there.

The trail quickly led them to the waterfront, where they learned that two men who gave themselves out as retired naval officers on a semi-official topographical expedition had hired a local fisherman earlier in the day to take them out to Broadmoor Island.

At first poor Wycroft, frustrated so often, almost lost his head. Almost did he rush along the wharf to hire another boat and give pursuit. But here the wiser counsels of Fielding prevailed.

"No, if they hired a local man to take them out and bring them back, there is no reason to think they will not be returning soon — within a day or so, as the man told his mates here," said Fielding. "But if we were to set out now, it might be our luck to have them come back early and go past us on the way, and be ashore and gone before we could put about and catch them. You heard what these men said, that Butcher hired the fastest sailing boat in the harbor. No, our rats are in a trap, and it behooves us to alert the authorities here — and then wait."

As difficult as it was simply to cool his heels on the wharf, Wycroft could not fail to see the wisdom of this course. So with two or three constables on call, ready to rally round the moment the fishing smack's mainsail was sighted in the distance, and with plenty of stout fisherfolk on hand as well to lend their aid if need be, Wycroft and Fielding took rooms in a waterfront tavern and settled down to wait.

This time Fortune was kinder. They did not have long to wait. To their great surprise they were called out in the early hours of the morning. The fishing smack had been sighted!

It was only with difficulty that Wycroft and Fielding

persuaded the onlookers and the constables who had been quickly summoned to stay out of sight until the boat was alongside the wharf, so as not to give her passengers the slightest cause for suspicion.

Swiftly the boat came toward the wharf through the dawn's early light, moving smartly in a freshening breeze. How eagerly Butcher must have been looking forward to setting foot on land and melting back into the anonymity of shore life! How hard Captain Wycroft's heart must have been beating as he wondered if he had come to the end of his long pursuit — or merely to another disappointment!

The boat came to the dock, headed up into the wind, and was laid expertly alongside by her master, while a couple of loungers — handpicked by Wycroft and instructed to say nothing out of the ordinary — took lines tossed to them by the fisherman and his passenger and made the boat fast. Thanking the fisherman gruffly and saying something about returning within a very few days, Butcher stepped off onto the dock.

As he did so, Wycroft and Fielding stepped forward.

"Good morning, sir," said Wycroft. "We would like a word with you."

Butcher looked startled. And then, as he noticed Fielding, he was visibly shaken.

Fielding stared hard at him.

"Sir, I believe I know you," he said in the accents of doomsday. "Beard or no beard, I'd stake my life on it! I know you!"

For once in his life Butcher panicked. For once he lost his head. He tried to break and run, but before he could get two steps he was seized and his arms were pinioned by two stout constables. He still struggled like the very devil, but in the end he was subdued.

On his person were found a pistol, which Wycroft, after sniffing its muzzle, declared had recently been fired, and a diamond and ruby necklace whose opulence made every onlooker gasp. Fielding guessed its origin at once.

"Taken from the Tyndalls, I'll be bound!" he growled.

When asked where his accomplice was, Butcher bared his teeth in a diabolical sneer.

"He's where you'll never find him!" he boasted, and would say no more.

"I reckon this pistol tells us where he is," said Wycroft, "but it's of no consequence — there's enough else to hang this bloody monster ten times over!"

Butcher and the necklace were both sent to England, though to quite separate destinations, to be sure. Butcher was sent back in chains, stood trial for his crimes, and was sentenced to hang.

The necklace was considered Crown property, but because of its great value a handsome reward was sent to the two captain-sleuths — a reward which Wycroft insisted should be Fielding's. With this capital in hand Fielding was now able to pay his share of expenses, and he yielded at last to his friend's entreaties to make the house in Barnham his permanent home. Today, friends to the end, the two men lie side by side in Barnham's historic burial ground.

But, you may say, this was supposed to be a ghost story! Yes, and so it is. But now, and only now, does that side of Captain Butcher's dreadful history finally come to the fore!

$\mathcal{O}$nce he was in prison and knew he was a doomed man, Butcher showed a streak of almost satanic glee. He began to talk freely and openly about his exploits — aye, boast openly about them! — to anyone who would listen. An intelligent warder named Higby was one of those who listened, and the account he wrote later of Captain Butcher's deeds and misdeeds is the original source of most of what we know of him.

Butcher took special delight in recounting the story of how he outwitted Jabez Tompkins, rejoicing in every detail.

"Dug his own grave, he did, after first digging up my box for me!" he always finished with a roar of laughter. "Saved me a lot of work, he did, the stupid fool!"

At the same time he began to have frequent nightmares in which he called out Tompkins's name, and when he awoke it was always with curses for Tompkins on his lips.

Now, among the other prisoners was an old man whom everyone called Crazy Smoots because he claimed to see visions and was given to making wild and often incoherent predictions. At times these seemed like the mere ravings of a madman, and yet many of the things he said had a way of coming true, so that the other prisoners were half afraid of him even though they laughed and jeered at him. Even the warder Higby writes of him with a certain awe and dread.

The night before Butcher was to be hanged Crazy Smoots was among a line of prisoners who shuffled past his cell. Suddenly the wild-eyed old man stopped and pointed a finger at Butcher.

"Every hundred years to the day!" he cried, "every hundred years to the day! I see it all, clear as clear can be — you'll go back there and murder him, every hundred years to the day, and in between you'll ne'er have a moment out o' the fiery pit — Old Scratch'll see to that!" he promised Butcher with a terrible, mirthless cackle.

It was said that Butcher turned deathly pale at the words and that he never smiled or spoke again from that moment on till the hangman's noose brought his misbegotten life to an end. In his account, Warder Higby reports a grisly jingle made up by prisoners at the time:

> *Captain Butcher's body*
> *Shall never lie at rest;*
> *Doomed is he each century*
> *To repeat his bloody jest!*

Eventually, of course, the story Butcher had told about his crime got back to Broadmoor Island and became a nine days' wonder there.

Enterprising souls dug up the small beach at the cove from one end to the other, but neither skeleton nor empty jewel casket was ever found. An eccentric

old fellow who lived a hermit's existence in a shanty near the cove took to showing off the area to visitors, pointing out the tower where Butcher had watched for Tompkins, and the spot on the beach where — according to the hermit, who by now had convinced himself he had witnessed the crime! — the murder had taken place. The old man began to refer to the cove as Butcher's Cove, and the name caught on.

The story became a prized legend on Broadmoor Island, of course, handed down from generation to generation. When a hundred years had passed, then, and July 11, 1846, was about to roll around, there were many who took note of the fact and began to speculate as to whether the prophecy of Crazy Smoots would come true. Would the ghost of Captain Butcher fulfill its horrid destiny and reenact the most notorious event of the island's history?

The hard-bitten seafaring folk of Broadmoor Island jested about it, of course, but at the same time they were, like most seamen, a superstitious lot and had seen enough strange and unaccountable things in their day to make them wonder.

Toward evening on July 11, almost shamefacedly, one inhabitant after another began to find excuses for drifting out in the direction of Butcher's Cove — shamefacedly, at least, until each of them noticed that practically the whole of the island's population seemed to be heading that way!

The result was much as might have been expected. Ghosts do not seem generally inclined to perform for crowds, preferring one or two onlookers at the most.

After quite a long wait, the last of the curious gave up and returned home disappointed.

As always, of course, there were attempts at practical jokes. Early arrivals that night found that someone had stuck a black-robed scarecrow up on the top of the tower. Then, a week or so later, two young boys came running home one evening full of a story of having seen ghosts on the beach — "one murthering t'other!" — but on close questioning they finally admitted they had not been near Butcher's Cove at all, but rather at an inlet a mile away along the shore. If those two jackanapes were not given a good hiding and sent to bed without any supper for having cried wolf for the mere devilment of it I don't know my crusty New Englanders!

And so endeth the strange and bloody history of Captain Butcher, a "ghost" who, so far as we know, has yet to walk the sands of Butcher's Cove where nearly two centuries ago he committed his foul crime. And yet, we wonder. In a few more years the second anniversary of the infamous murder will roll around, and we wonder. Was Crazy Smoots wrong, or was Captain Butcher really on hand back on the night of July 11, 1846 — on hand to keep his grisly date with Destiny, but there in a form unseen by the rustic curiosity-seekers?

On the night of July 11, 1946, will the story be a different one?

I for one intend to be on hand at Butcher's Cove that night — without, I hope, too many companions!

4

Butcher's Cove

Seven

Well, as Marshall Watkins himself had written, it was not much of a ghost story — a story without a ghost, in fact — but otherwise it left nothing to be desired as far as I was concerned.

Closing the book, but still under the spell of the story, I experienced one of those magical moments when everything around you takes on new dimensions, when everything looks different from the way it did the last time you looked. It was here, here! This was the place, this island. An actual pirate ship had anchored off this island, an extraordinary murder had taken place here! That much was true, at least, whether Captain Butcher's ghost ever walked or not.

A breeze went whispering through the trees and the grass around me, and voices from the past were in it.

Captain Butcher must have passed close by to where I was sitting on his way to the place where he would lie in wait for Jabez Tompkins. Tompkins, too, had climbed this hill on his way to sudden death. No house was here then, no house or barn, only a barren hilltop with the rough moors rolling away beyond it.

A sense of the past being near, of past, present, and future flowing together, of time collapsing like an accordion, became so vivid that it made my heart thump as though some invisible force were enveloping me. I scrambled to my feet in a conscious effort to break the spell; the present seemed to snap back into place. All the same, a new ingredient had been added to the atmosphere of my island, and it was there to stay.

Now, of course, I was eager to talk to someone about what I had read. For a moment I hesitated, looking uncertainly toward Leo's tent. He had let me read the story; maybe he would be willing to talk about it.

Then I remembered he had told me to give the book to my father, as Aunt Fanny had asked him to, so I decided I had better do that first.

I went inside and upstairs to the room where Dad was trying to settle down to work. Several crumpled sheets of paper were in and around the wastebasket, and he was staring at a blank sheet in the typewriter when I came in.

"Here's that book about Captain Butcher, Dad. Leo said to give it to you, but he said I could read it first if I wanted to, so I did. Wait till you read it! It's great!"

Dad glanced up, looking irritated, but secretly welcoming any excuse to escape for a moment from the struggle to get started again on his book.

"All right, put it there," he snapped, pointing to a corner of his worktable, still trying to pretend to himself I had interrupted a productive train of thought. But then he cocked a sardonic eyebrow my way. "You're all set to go ghost-hunting, I suppose."

"Well, the ghost part isn't much — but the pirate stuff is nifty!"

"Fine. Just what I need to inspire me, a good pirate story," grumbled Dad. Then to his sardonic expression he added a puckery grin. "By the way, I see you found someone to play catch with."

"Yeah! Who'd ever have thought Leo could throw like that?"

"Who'd have thought Leo could throw at all? Well, I'm glad he condescended to act like a boy for a change. Thank him for the book," said Dad, and gave it the tempted look of a compulsive reader. He reached his hand out for it in the guilty way a fat man reaches for a dish of peanuts.

"Well . . . I'll have a look at it. I might as well take a break for a few minutes, anyway . . ."

"It's Chapter Four," I told him, and left him riffling through the pages to find his place.

Now I had a legitimate excuse for interrupting whatever Leo might be doing. I had to tell him Dad thanked him for the book, didn't I? I ran into trouble on my way outside, however. Mom met me in the hall.

"George, come in here," she said, pointing to my room.

"What's the matter, Mom?"

"Just take a look at this room. That's what's the matter. Now, you're not to scatter your things all over the place, and especially not on the other bed —"

"Well, gee, Mom, why not?"

"Because that is Leo's bed, if he chooses to use it, and some night when it's cold and rainy he may want to do just that."

There are about a million things mothers never seem to understand, and one of them is that any normal boy, even Leo — especially Leo, considering how stubborn he could be — any normal boy would lie outside in his tent and drown by inches before he would come inside just because it was raining. But I had to spend time neatening up the place, and for what? Well, the real reason was not what Mom said at all. The real reason was that then Aunt Gladys couldn't look in the room and find something to criticize. I know that now, but how was I to know it then?

It was quite a while before I got outside.

When finally I looked in through the opening of his tent, Leo was staring thoughtfully at a pad of scratch paper. He had a pencil in his hand.

"Hi, Leo. Dad said to thank you for the book."

Leo grunted.

"I read it first," I added. "It was great!"

Another grunt. My visit to Leo's tent was beginning to sound like a visit to a pigsty, except that no pig was ever this fussy about his sty, with a place for everything and everything in its place. Leo even had little shelves set up for his books!

I stared down at the scratch pad in his lap.

"What's that?"

He snuffled in a breath and pursed his lips.

"It's none of your business." Having established that point to his own offensive satisfaction, he added, "But I'll tell you anyway. It's a map."

"A map? What of?"

"Butcher's Cove."

"You drew it yourself?"

"Certainly."

"Oh. You've already been out there, huh?"

This took the wind out of my sails a bit. Actually, I had been thinking that maybe . . . And I had thought that maybe Leo might . . .

"Which bike do you use?" I asked next.

"Blue one."

"Okay, then I'll use the red one."

"Where do you think you're going?" he retorted in a lazy, lofty tone. "It's a tough ride down to the village — at least it's plenty tough coming back, pumping up that hill."

"I wasn't thinking about going down there. I was thinking about . . . Well, how far is it to Butcher's Cove?"

Leo's small mouth twitched.

"Story hooked you, did it?"

"It was terrific!"

Another grunt.

"It's okay," he allowed.

I glanced at the map again and asked a question with suitable humility, an approach I figured might best get me an answer from this weird and exasperating cousin of mine.

"Can you tell me how to get out there, Leo?"

He frowned, glared around in an irritably thoughtful way, and sighed.

"Oh, you'd never find it on your own," he snapped scornfully. "I guess I might as well go out there again too. There's a couple of things I want to check up on for my map."

"Great! I'll go put on some sneakers, and —"

"I want to take my field glasses. I left them in the house. Bring — no, never mind, I'll get them myself. I know where they are."

I rushed ahead to find my sneakers. When I came out of my room after putting them on I heard voices down the hall in Dad's workroom. The voices were his and Leo's. Surprised, I went to the door and looked in.

"What did you think of it, Uncle Paul?" Leo was asking in a very formal voice. It was plain they were being stand-offish, sort of sniffing around each other like two strange dogs who didn't care for one another but who had decided to be polite for the present. Afterward I found out that Leo had left his field glasses in the bay window at the end of the hall, which forced him to pass Dad's door, and that Dad had called him in, feeling he ought to thank him for the book. One of those things. So now Leo was asking Dad what he thought of the story, and Dad was pulling on his pipe and preparing his critical appraisal.

"Well, Watkins is a terrible writer in places, what with that 'Shiver our timbers!' opening and the 'torrid climes of the Caribbean Sea' stuff and a few other such touches, but once he gets going he tells a good story."

Leo looked primly pleased. It was obvious the criticism rang a bell with him. He nodded in pompous agreement.

"He's a windbag. Uses a lot of tautology —"

Dad pricked up his ears at that one.

"Tautology? Where did you pick up that term, Leo?"

Leo shrugged, fighting self-consciousness.

"My English teacher is death on that stuff."

"Stuff like 'gather together' and 'original source,'" said Dad, quoting a couple of Marshall Watkins's contributions to the field. If he had wanted to impress Leo — and I think he did — he could not have chosen a better way. Leo blinked.

"That's right! And how about 'crouched down'?"

"Bull's-eye! That's one I missed!" said Dad magnanimously, because he was enjoying himself now at one of his favorite sports. Dad was one of those word nuts. He loved nothing better than to talk about words. And Leo! Dad's reception of "crouched down" left him positively pink with pleasure.

"What's wrong with 'crouched down'?" I demanded almost defiantly.

Leo turned to me, and for the first time there was a glint of pure fun in his eyes.

"Let's see you crouch *up,*" he said, and savored my

father's chuckle. "And when things are gathered they can't be anything but together, so you don't have to use both words."

"And a source *has* to be original," added Dad. "In other words, tautology is the art of needless repetition."

I was beginning to resent these caviling criticisms of Marshall Watkins's exciting prose — and also, perhaps, to feel a bit jealous of the way Leo and Dad were suddenly getting along.

"Well, I don't care about *that* stuff," I cried. "*I* think it's the best story I've ever read!"

Dad laughed, but a pat on my shoulder and his next words made me feel better.

"You bet it is, son! The man's a storyteller, I'll give him that."

Leo pursed his lips, still determined to be disdainful.

"But do you think he's accurate, Uncle Paul?"

"Hmm. Well, Leo, I don't know. A slapdash writer is liable to be a slapdash researcher as well. For instance, I remember reading something about Broadmoor in England, and I'm almost sure the insane asylum wasn't established there until long after Broadmoor Island had been named. On the other hand, Newgate *was* a prison by then, and had been for centuries. Well, I suppose those are small points. I expect his important details can be trusted. Still, I'd certainly like to read the original account that warder at the prison wrote — what was his name? Higby?"

"So would I," agreed Leo. "The next time I get to

Boston I'm going to the library and see if they have it."

I was becoming impatient with all this nitpicking literary talk.

"Well, come on, Leo, let's go out there," I urged.

He automatically started to snap at me but then held his tongue, obviously in deference to Dad. For Leo this was something. Progress in human relations. And by then Dad was asking me a question.

"Where are you going, George?"

"Out to Butcher's Cove. Leo's going to show me how to get there. He's made a map of it!"

"Oh? I'd like to see it."

"Well, I want to check a couple of things, to be sure I've got them absolutely right," said Leo in very weighty tones, "but when we get back and I've made any necessary changes I'll show it to you, Uncle Paul."

"Fine."

With that we finally took off and headed for the barn and the bikes, both of us with plenty to think about.

I was torn two ways: still jealous of how Leo had been able to talk with Dad sort of man-to-man, but pleased with the way Leo had become, at least for a few moments, less surly and more human. As for Leo, he had an odd, surprised expression on his face, and it is not hard now to guess why.

He was surprised to find he was beginning to like his uncle.

Eight

In those days most of the people on Broadmoor Island still lived in the village or, like Aunt Fanny and a few others, on the top of the rise just above. I shouldn't call it a hill, because beyond Aunt Fanny's place the island stayed high, falling away again near the shore on the southeasterly side. Beyond Aunt Fanny's the land rolled in broad, bare reaches in all directions, barren, windswept, and empty, with a sky so vast it made me feel like an ant crawling along under it.

Since then I have seen the moors of the Scottish highlands and know that, as Marshall Watkins said, Broadmoor really does look the way they do, just as wild, as treeless, as lonely. For the most part, the only visible sign that the island might be inhabited was the dirt road, little more than two tracks, that made a wobbly circuit of the island without coming near the shore at more than one or two points. I wondered if the road had been in existence when Captain Butcher tramped this way. Had the dust my bike tires were leaving their treadmarks on once shaped itself into his footprints?

Our course took us across the southerly side of the island. I pedaled along behind Leo, getting used to the red bike, listening to the hiss of the tires on the gritty, hard-packed sand surface of the tracks, reveling in the sunshine and the sea breeze that swept the open land. After about a mile the road dipped down a gentle slope toward the sea, then seemed to think better of it, climbing back up out of the broad hollow near the shore and gradually turning inland again. A few minutes later Leo stopped.

"This is as close as the road comes to Butcher's Cove. From here on we walk."

Even though it had climbed a bit, the road was still following a fold in the moors that was like the trough between two waves at sea, so that during that stretch nothing of the coastline was visible. I could understand now why Leo had said I would not be able to find the cove by myself. He took his scratch pad out of his handlebar basket and put it under his arm. Leaving the bikes beside the road, we climbed the southerly slope.

One moment things looked pretty much the same in every direction. A couple of minutes later we topped the rise and everything was laid out ahead of us as clearly as if I had been looking at Leo's map.

Ahead of us the moors rolled in long dips and swells down to the sea. Not more than half a mile away the sickle sweep of a cove bit into the shore with only the corners of its beach visible because of the bluff that rose above it. To the right of the cove, rugged and gray, a stone tower tied together the sky and sea, cutting across the horizon about midway up its height.

Leo swept his hand across the scene with a more dramatic gesture than I would have expected of him.

"Well, there it is. Butcher's Cove," he said, and though he tried to keep his voice flat I could tell he was stirred, even excited.

And I? Need I say that my imagination was hard at work, putting a black pirate ship at anchor in the center of the cove, seeing darkness settle around it, hearing the men carousing until all but Butcher and Tompkins were snoring in drunken slumber, and then seeing a dark figure slip over the side into a small boat?

Of course Leo had to find something to be critical about.

"If you ask me, Butcher didn't mind taking fool chances!"

"Like what?"

"Like putting in here at all, when he had a chart of the island and must have known there were dangerous shoals east of the cove. I'll bet he sneaked her in from well to the southwest, and took her out again on the same course, or as close to it as he could," said Leo, revealing himself as at least an armchair sailor. I learned later that he actually had done some sailing and was pretty good at it, in that irritating way he had of being good at most things he tried. "Still, the place was ideal for his purpose, and that's why he took the chance. Come on, let's go down."

When I say the cove was not more than half a mile distant, I mean the way we were looking, as the crow flies. The way we walked it, up and down the rolling moors, was more like a mile, and not an easy mile, either. But I would not have minded twice the distance that day.

Each time we topped a rise the cove was nearer, and each time I thought, this is the place where real pirates came in a real pirate ship, and I'm here! And in a few minutes I would be looking down at the very spot where Captain Butcher stepped out from behind a boulder and put a bullet into Jabez Tompkins's head, and Tompkins fell forward into his grave.

Such thoughts were more than enough to keep me going, even though Leo with his longer legs set a cruel pace. Furthermore, off to the right of the cove there was the stone tower to think about, the grim pillar of jagged-edged stonework atop which Captain Butcher had kept his murderous watch while Jabez Tompkins picked his way across the moors with his dark lantern and his spade. It was all richly satisfying to a boy who so recently had been reveling in the enthusiastic prose of Marshall Watkins.

"What's a dark lantern, Leo?" I asked out of the blue. His mouth twitched.

"Thinking about Tompkins, huh?"

As usual, Leo knew the answer, and gave it in words close enough to a dictionary definition to make me suspect now that he had looked it up.

"It's a lantern with only one opening, and that one can be closed to hide the light."

At last we reached the edge of the low bluff and looked down on the beach below. The actual sand beach was small, extending not more than fifty yards along the inner edge of the cove. The rest of the beach was a jumble of rocks and pebbles. Down on the beach a couple of boulders sat heavily on the wet sand, but neither of them was very impressive. The larger was only about five feet high.

"How did he hide behind *those?*" I wondered. "He really must have had to crouch down — to crouch."

Leo smirked at my avoidance of tautology, but he nodded.

"It doesn't look like much of a hiding place. But remember, you're looking at it in broad daylight. When Butcher was hiding there it was pitch dark. Besides, in those days the average person was much shorter than today, and that would make a difference."

We climbed down the bluff to the beach, where Leo began pacing off distances between the boulders and various other points and checking directions carefully with a pocket compass. During this process he gave me the pad to hold. Once in a while he would come over to jot a notation on it. He managed to make the whole procedure look very scientific. Finally he paused at a point about five paces from the larger boulder.

"I figure Tompkins must have been standing some-where near here," he said.

I walked over toward him and we both stared down at the smooth sand between us, visualizing the dark pit . . .

"But they never found anything," I said.

"Why should they? In a hundred years, with the tides going in and out every day, and lots of storms, the sand could hide anything — shift it around, bury it deeper —"

"But it wasn't a hundred years later when all those people dug up the beach, it was only a little while later, when the news got back about the story Captain Butcher had told!" I cried triumphantly. "Don't you remember?"

Leo's face went pink, and not with pleasure.

"Oh — er — well . . . well, sure! . . ."

He was furious at having been caught in a slip of memory. His self-esteem had suffered a blow. I ex-pected him to take it out on me with some nasty retort, and was prepared to dislike him all the more for it, when to my surprise he took it out on himself instead.

"How stupid can I get?"

His forehead took such a punishing rap from his knuckles that I could see him wince. Then he looked at me in a different way and his face twisted into some-thing more like a real grin than I had ever seen there before.

"You surprise me! You're thinking!" he said, and despite his attempt to make the words sound sarcastic I felt as if I had had a medal pinned on me. "Well, anyway, let's see, now . . ."

Frowning down at the sand, he wrestled with this new problem.

"How long would it have been before word got back here about Butcher's story? . . . Even then, not more than a year. So why didn't they find anything when they dug up the beach? Maybe a freak storm, a really big one, had torn up the beach by then."

"You mean, enough to uncover the body and wash it away?"

"It's possible, if there was a hurricane. The exposure's just right. I'll have to see if there is any record of a big gale or a hurricane that year. Or maybe . . ." His eyes lighted up and he nodded, better pleased now with his own thinking apparatus. "Yes, maybe someone else had already done some digging. That old hermit, maybe."

"You mean, you think he really did see —"

"No. He may have been a hermit, but he doesn't sound so nutty that he wouldn't have come running to town with the news if he had really seen anything. But he might have passed the cove a day or so later and noticed a hump in the sand that didn't look natural — I doubt if Butcher bothered to smooth everything out when he got through burying Tompkins. So maybe the hermit got curious and did some digging."

"But if he dug up the body, wouldn't he let people know what he'd found?"

Leo thought that over for a moment, putting to-

116

gether ideas, drawing on what he had read as much as what he had observed.

"Hermits are hermits because they don't like people and don't trust them," he said finally, and managed to sound every bit as weighty and authoritative as Moses reading off the Ten Commandments. "Anyone who finds a body when there's obviously been foul play becomes an automatic suspect himself, and I'll bet the old boy thought of that — if he *did* find the body, that is."

"Then what did he do with it?"

"Got rid of it. He could have — Oh, listen, he probably didn't find it anyway, so we're just wasting time talking about it!"

"Well, either a hurricane or that old hermit must have dug it up, because it wasn't there. Marshall Watkins says they dug up the beach from one end to the other —"

"Oh, baloney!" said Leo, suddenly finding a new argument. "That's just the kind of overstatement you can expect from a blowhard like him! Take a look at that beach! Can you imagine anyone really digging up every square foot of it from one end to the other?"

This time Leo had really come up with something. It was obvious the realization had just hit him; he had not stopped to think about it before, but that did not make it any the less effective. A statement claiming that people dug up the beach "from one end to the other" was one of those exaggerations that breeze right past us on paper. I had to admit my faith in Marshall Watkins was shaken as Leo pressed his argument home.

"Sure, I can imagine people deciding here might be a good place, or there, and digging a hole here and there — but the whole beach? It would take a gang of men a week to do that. Maybe if they had thought a fortune was buried there they might have done it, but nobody's going to dig that hard just for a skeleton and an empty box!"

"I guess you're right," I conceded, and then thrilled to the thought that inevitably popped next into my mind. "But if that's how it was, then maybe the body is still here!"

"Maybe." He looked at me then, and his eyes were actually twinkling. He looked almost human. "You want to spend your summer digging up the beach? Go right ahead. I'll hold your coat."

I grinned, and Cousin Leo grinned. He handed me the pencil.

"Okay, now, I want to check a few more things, and you can write down what I tell you," he said, and from then on I was part of the operation.

When he had taken care of the beach to his satisfaction we climbed the bluff again, and he led the way to the tower. We stood looking up its rough-hewn, weathered height.

"Want to climb up inside?"

"Sure!"

Another teasing grin appeared.

"Captain Butcher's ghost may be up there."

The very suggestion sent a delicious thrill up my spine — delicious because it was totally vicarious — and I answered with great bravado.

"I'll take my chances."

"Huh! You wouldn't be so cocky if it was pitch dark."

"You wouldn't be, either!" I sauced him back recklessly. Leo's grin disappeared. I thought he was going to get stuffy again, or even mad. But instead he turned to stare up at the tower with a glance that had gone dark and inward. When he replied he spoke with a sort of hard honesty.

"Maybe not. I don't know. It would depend . . ."

Then he jerked his head at me.

"Come on."

Inside the tower a rough circular staircase mounted to a flat platform surrounded by a parapet about four feet high. After more than two centuries there was still a hint of blackness about the surface of the gray stones, a faint but indelibly imprinted memory of all the fires that had once blazed up there. In the bright sunshine, however, with the sea sparkling below us, the tower seemed little more than a pleasant lookout.

"Well, if Captain Butcher's ghost is hanging around here, *I* wouldn't know it," I said, cocky again.

Leo gave the situation one of his gravely considered appraisals and began to talk in the bookish jargon he so often affected.

"I don't feel any psychic sensations, either, not the kind described by reliable witnesses in some of the well-documented cases," he declared in that pedantic tone of voice that made people want to kick him in the pants — pompous, self-consciously serious. Just as I was wishing I were old enough and big enough to do the kicking, however, his tone changed in a way that was easier to live with. "But why should we feel anything here and now, at this time of day, and three days before he's supposed to be here? He'd be pretty dumb if he started watching for Jabez Tompkins three days ahead of time!"

This was more like it.

"He'd get pretty hungry," I pointed out.

"He wouldn't be the only one. I'm hungry right now," said Leo, suddenly reminded.

"You and me, too!" I said, just as suddenly aware that my own stomach had inspired my last remark. "Let's go!"

In an atmosphere that was positively companionable we turned to leave, but after a few steps Leo stopped to look back at the tower. Once again his dark, deep-set eyes brooded both outwardly and inwardly.

"I wonder just how scared I *would* be . . ."

Words burst out of me before I could stop them.

"Well, you were sure brave that time when . . ."

Leo's eyes snapped in my direction as I broke off, aghast. I had mentioned the unmentionable. But it was the open admiration my words contained that shook Leo up the most. Instead of feeling resentment, he found himself grappling with complicated emotions that took him by surprise. Dislike, envy, ridicule — Leo was used to all those responses to his difficult personality. He was always ready to deal with them and give as good as he got or better. But to find himself admired for his courage was something he was not prepared for. He went red with embarrassment, and tried to think of what to say. Once again, he plumped for honesty.

"Listen, I *was* scared . . ."

"Maybe so. But you didn't run."

Leo had to look away, so he looked at the tower again.

"Well . . . who knows? Anyway, you're going to see some running right now, because if we don't get home soon I'll starve to death!"

With that he took off, and we ran till we were out of breath. But this time he held the pace down so that I could keep up with him.

Nine

The next three days were a period of mounting irritation for Leo and me.

Aunt Fanny drove down to the village every morning to do her shopping, and occasionally went down on other errands at other times of day. During the period preceding Butcher's Cove Day, as they had started calling it locally, she never came back from one of her trips without some news that set our teeth on edge.

"Otis Hinckley's going to drive his family out."

"The Doanes are planning to take a picnic."

"Joe Feeny's fixing to sail round to the cove with a bunch of folks if the weather holds."

From the sound of things it was going to be worse than back in 1846. Leo was burned up.

"A picnic! That's — that's —"

"You mark my words," said Dad, "some people will take a picnic to see the end of the world. When the whole place goes up in flames, somebody will be eating a hamburger."

Next came national publicity. In those days there was a weekly magazine called *Liberty*. The day before Butcher's Cove Day the mailboat brought over copies of the latest edition of *Liberty* with an article in it by Marshall Watkins entitled "The Ghost of Butcher's Cove."

In it he retold the story of Captain Butcher — lifting most of it word for word from his own book — and concluded with a few jaunty observations about Crazy Smoots's prediction:

> One thing you can say for Crazy Smoots — at the very worst he's going to be wrong once every hundred years, and how many of us are wrong that seldom?
>
> Captain Butcher did not show up back in 1846. If he disappoints us again in 1946 I may have to retitle this article "The World's Worst Ghost Story." On the other hand, maybe we Butcher fans should try to cultivate the kind of diehard optimism the Brooklyn Dodger fans have. Every time the Dodgers finish last again in the National League the Dodgers fans say, "Wait till next year!" Maybe we Butcher fans should say, "Wait till 2046!"

It was pretty plain, even before he showed up, that Marshall Watkins did not expect to see anything unusual out at Butcher's Cove.

When the big day came Aunt Fanny announced she would drive anyone to the scene that wanted to go. Of course Leo and I were going on our own, on our bikes.

"I'll walk up to where we can see the cove," said Aunt Fanny, "but I don't think I'll haul these old bones all the way down there and back."

The whole family decided to go. Mom and Aunt Gladys said they would stay with Aunt Fanny. Dad said he might walk down to the cove for a look.

Shortly before suppertime Aunt Fanny and Dad took a spin down to the village with the frank intention of nosing around. They came back with several pieces of news.

"Marshall Watkins is here. Came over on the afternoon boat. Asa Bearse is going to drive him out in his Studebaker."

Asa Bearse was both our town constable and one of the town selectmen, the nearest thing Broadmoor Island had to a prominent politician.

"We're being honored by another distinguished visitor," my father added, "a man named Whitney. He's the president of something called the Society for the Investigation of Psychic Phenomena."

"In other words, a spook hunter," said Aunt Fanny, causing a stuffy look of disapproval to cross Leo's face like a cloud. The look was ignored by the speaker —

though slyly appreciated, I suspect — as she moved on to another news flash.

"Joe Feeny's sail is off, though. Joe took a look at the weather and said it's going to rain buckets before the night's out."

This was the only piece of news to which Leo gave any welcome.

"I hope it *does* rain!" he muttered. "Maybe then the crowd will stay away!"

We ate a little early, and then it was time for Leo and me to get started — in fact, he had been on pins and needles all through supper and had gobbled his food at such a rate that Aunt Fanny made him slow down.

"Don't want you to choke to death and have *your* ghost walking around here burping, Leo," she told him.

She made us sit around for a few minutes after supper "to let our food settle," and even Leo could not do anything against Aunt Fanny's iron will. But finally we were released, and we raced out to our bikes.

Over toward the west the sky *was* tending to frown a little, but with a boy's optimism I decided it probably wouldn't rain enough to spoil things — maybe just enough to scare all the other people off, the way we hoped.

Before we reached the stretch of road nearest Butcher's Cove, however, two or three cars had already passed us, two of them with whooping kids in them, and just before we got there Aunt Fanny caught up with us.

The Doanes were already on hand, seven strong, having their picnic up on the hillside. Leo's face went taut with outrage. He climbed the hill, giving them a wide berth as though they were lepers, while Aunt Fanny and the others passed them at a more sociable distance to say hello. I of course followed in Leo's footsteps.

When we were partway up we heard another car coming. Asa Bearse's Studebaker. Beside Asa in the front seat was a large, hearty man with a mane of gray hair and a red face. He was holding forth in a booming voice — in fact, he sounded as if he had his own loudspeaker system built into his larynx — and there was barely room enough in the car for his gestures, the product of years spent on the lecture circuit. In the back seat, sitting straight as a ramrod, was a cadaverous old gentleman clutching a rolled umbrella as if it were a weapon.

"That's Watkins in front," said Aunt Fanny, hardly surprising any of us. "I see he still likes to talk as much as ever. The dried-up specimen in back is the spook hunter. If you ask me, all he needs to do to find one is to look in the mirror."

Leo surveyed the whole scene with irascible distaste, unquestionably considering himself a lone Deep Thinker in a desert of brainless vulgarity. Ahead of us, a few people were already straggling down the moors toward the cove.

"Let's go!" Leo muttered to me in an impatient undertone.

Aunt Fanny cast a sharp eye at the heavens.

"You youngsters keep a lookout on the weather," she ordered. "I don't know but what Joe Feeny's right."

"I'm going to wait and say hello to our celebrities," said Dad. We left him with our womenfolk.

The sun had set long ago behind a bank of thick gray clouds. By the time we reached the cove it was dusk, and Charter Light was beginning to wink at us from the distant mainland.

Leo had hardly a word to say all the way down to the cove. He was too busy feeling disgusted. It was when we got there, however, that his disgust really came into its own. Several people were sitting along the edge of the bluff. Down on the beach half a dozen kids were frolicking around.

"Those ———s!" Leo used a word that would have gotten him into serious trouble at home. His eyes were burning, his face was flushed, and he was clenching and unclenching his big fists. If he could have had his way right then I think there would have been several more murders down on the beach. "Look at them — tramping around, messing up everything — there ought to be a law!"

He flung himself down on a clump of beach grass and banged his fist on the ground, wild with helpless rage. It seemed like a good time to say nothing, and for once I did. I kept quiet and waited for him to simmer down.

Just to add a final touch, the Doane kids came whooping across the dunes and joined the others on the beach. Then, before long, four more figures came into view. Selectman Bearse, Marshall Watkins, Mr. Whitney, and Dad. Asa Bearse immediately began to throw his weight around, and to some effect.

"Here, you kids, get off that beach!" he shouted. "Mr. Whitney here wants to do some investigating, and he doesn't need you underfoot!"

The kids made a few faces and grumbled about their rights, but they obeyed. Asa Bearse could be high-handed when he felt like it, and he was perfectly capable of kicking their pants off the beach personally if they gave him any trouble. They came up to roost on the edge of the bluff with the other onlookers and to watch Mr. Whitney, who now put on a performance of his own.

Moving in a precise, fussy, thoroughly determined way, and still armed with his umbrella, the gaunt old gentleman sidestepped down the face of the bluff and began to stalk around the beach like an inquisitive heron.

Here and there he went, poking at the sand now and then with his umbrella in much the same way a shore bird might poke his bill into it. Presently he clambered slowly up the bluff again and marched over to the tower. He disappeared inside, was seen briefly on the top platform, then came down again. He walked back toward the other men with a discouraging expression on his long face.

"I am what is known as a sensitive," he announced with complete assurance. "I am sensitive to psychic phenomena. I have proved this on numerous occasions. I sense nothing here, however. Nothing at all. I am afraid you are in for a disappointment, gentlemen. Since it looks very much as if it may rain before long, I shall wait for you in the car."

With that Mr. Whitney set his course nor'-nor'west with never a backward glance. And as though by way of agreeing with him, thunder rumbled in the south. Asa Bearse glanced around uneasily.

"Wind's come around to the sou'east. That means rain for sure. I don't hanker to get caught down here in a gully-washer, besides which the road ain't much to drive on when it gets slippery-wet."

Marshall Watkins took the clue. Tossing his mane of gray hair, he gathered eyes.

"Gentlemen," he said in his resonant, lecture-hall voice, "I think Mr. Whitney and Mr. Bearse are right. Before it gets much darker we're going to have the kind of weather no sensible ghost would be caught dead in. I think we can safely conclude that Captain Butcher is going to misfire again. I move we join Mr. Whitney."

Dad glanced over at us.

"I suppose you two are determined to stay. Well, Aunt Fanny says a little rain never hurt boys — so long as they have a good hot bath afterward, so be prepared. I can tell you from experience she means it."

"If you see anything interesting be sure to let me know, boys!" said Marshall Watkins with a jovial wink.

"Okay," said Leo, without sounding too enthusiastic. A few of the other onlookers had already gathered up their kids and headed back, and now the rest of them decided to keep the visiting celebrity company. We were going to have the place to ourselves after all! On the other hand, there could no longer be much doubt about the weather. It was going to rain cats and dogs.

I turned to Leo.

"What do you think?"

"We can take cover if we have to."

"Where?"

He jerked his head in the direction of the tower.

"Let's go have a look."

By now twilight had cast a thick haze over everything. This was the time when Captain Butcher must have been up on the platform, on the lookout for Jabez Tompkins. As we stood there alone, the mere suggestion of going in there should have been enough to turn me into quivering jelly. But it didn't. As I followed Leo inside the tower I felt nothing that frightened me. It merely seemed like a good place to get in out of the rain.

Leo looked around him and shook his head in a dispirited way.

"I was interested in what Mr. Whitney said about being a sensitive. I think we can believe that he really is one," he declared in a weighty, judicious tone of voice. "And I think he was right. This place is about as exciting as a bus stop!"

Having checked our shelter we went outside to wait for the rain to come and to watch the beach below us. Lightning flashed in the distance, thunder rolled across the dark waters with a hollow rumble. The whole sky was black and stormy now. Grand opera could not have produced a more sinister setting. Everything that should have made the atmosphere creepy was doing its bit, and yet the essential ingredient was missing.

Evil.

Try as we might, neither of us could work up the slightest sensation of impending evil, of something terrible about to happen.

A few big spatters of rain warned us that the storm was arriving. We retreated into the tower just as total darkness and the downpour seemed to sweep ashore together.

It was a crash-bang affair of the first order, that storm. Rain came down in such torrents as to blot out everything around us — the moors, the dunes, the cove, the sea, and the beach below us.

Since the tower entrance faced away from the sea we couldn't have seen the beach from there anyway, but that didn't matter. *Anything* could have been going on down there without our seeing or hearing it even if we had gone outside. So we sat inside the tower and then rose and stood huddled against the curved walls as rainwater began to cascade down the stone stairs. We not only saw and heard nothing, but worse yet, we *felt* nothing — except rain dripping down our necks.

"Once in a hundred years, and it has to pick tonight

to rain like this!" raged Leo, glaring out at the boisterous storm with a hatred that almost equaled the glares he had lavished on the kids on the beach.

"I wish the rain would stop so we could go home," I grumbled, beginning to think of the long walk back across the moors and the long ride on a muddy road on wet bicycles.

"You can go if you want to, but I'm staying," snapped Leo in a stubborn voice. "This is only a thunderstorm. It'll soon be over. And when it is I want to watch the beach a while longer."

"Well . . . okay. But I wish it would saw off."

It didn't. Instead, after what seemed like hours, the rain settled into a thick, steady drizzle that looked as if it might go on forever. Even Leo had to admit it was not a fit night out for ghosts or anyone else, and finally he did, though of course not in so many words.

"Oh, there's no use hanging around here any longer, it's getting too late!" he said. "If Marshall Watkins is right, it hadn't been dark long when Jabez Tompkins got to the beach. By now the murder would have taken place."

The look on his face would have been worthy of Napoleon the moment he finally realized there was no point in hanging around Moscow any longer, and that a long, uncomfortable retreat lay ahead of him.

"Let's go," said Leo.

Unhooking a flashlight from his belt he led the way outside, hunching his shoulders against the rain. I followed in his sodden footsteps. Halfway back to the

133

road he slipped and dropped the flashlight. Its bulb broke. We had to stumble along in the dark the rest of the way.

By then most sections of the road were either mushy where there was sand or slippery where there was clay, so that we had to walk our bikes most of the way home.

As we plodded along Leo could find only one bleak bit of comfort in the situation.

"Well, anyway, we were the only ones who stayed!"

And so ended Butcher's Cove Day. Dad was right about those hot baths, too. We got them, about three minutes after we came dragging in.

To tell the truth, I don't think either of us really minded. Furthermore, that night Leo slept in the house, in that other bed in my room. Not without some protests on his part, to be sure, but they were pretty feeble. And if he wasn't just as glad to climb into bed as I was, I'll eat my cap, bill and all.

Ten

In the morning Leo was sour and sulky, still suffering from the previous night's disappointments. It was all he could do to say good morning at breakfast, and I don't think he would have done that if it were not for the fact that nobody sat down at Aunt Fanny's breakfast table without saying good morning to everybody else.

Aunt Gladys was sure, of course, that her poor Leo would have a cold, and of course Leo disappointed her by not having one at all.

"Did 'em both good. Both look cleaner than they have for ages," said Aunt Fanny. "It's too bad Captain Butcher let you down, though."

A painful sound issued from Leo. It could have been intended for a bitter laugh.

"Captain Butcher!" He spoke his next words in the portentous tones of a judge about to hand down a death sentence. "I agree with Mr. Whitney. I didn't feel a thing out there last night. Not one thing."

"Ah, Mr. Whitney. What a character!" said Dad fondly. "I loved the way he marched off to the car, umbrella at the ready. But he was a lot more interesting than he might have seemed. Let me just give you a report on Mr. Whitney. It may interest Leo.

"I'll hand him one thing, Mr. Whitney is a serious investigator, and he doesn't give a tinker's dam whether people laugh at him or listen to him. He's not a nut, or a fanatic. There's nothing romantic or credulous about his attitude toward ghosts. His approach is quite different.

"He feels there is nothing supernatural about the possibility of ghosts, since in a sense — he says — we are *all* ghosts.

"We think of our bodies as solid, physical objects made of solid flesh and bone, but this is an illusion, because actually we are a conglomeration of minute particles, billions and billions of electrons circling nuclei at relatively great distances with the speed of light. All these eventually leave our bodies as cells 'die' and are replaced by others, so that we are never quite the same collection of particles from one instant to the next. Not a trace of the cells that made up our bodies seven years ago remains a part of us today. All have been replaced by new ones.

"Now, if all those tiny particles can come and go that way, says Mr. Whitney, why shouldn't a group needed to form a particular body be able to reassemble for a short time if the pull is strong enough? He believes that every particle has memory stored in it, just as memory is stored in those new machines scientists are working on, those computers. That being the case, the cells can come together again, each in its old place, and re-create the body briefly.

"How do you like that for a theory?"

Dad sat back from the table and enjoyed our various expressions.

Aunt Fanny's brow was wrinkled over the wrinkles, giving the theory a good try. Aunt Gladys's pretty face was vacant, as if she had gotten lost quite a way back. Mom's attitude was that of an unbeliever who is willing to listen. And at the same time everyone was sliding glances in Leo's direction, wondering how he was going to take it.

His face was as wooden as a poker player's, but dark fires were stirring in his eyes. And in a way he turned the tables on us by answering a question with a question.

"How do *you* like it, Uncle Paul?"

Dad smiled, and shrugged.

"Somehow I think Mr. Whitney made it sound more believable than I have, maybe because of his own sense of conviction. But it's — well, it's interesting."

"There are scientists who would agree with him," said Leo. "I've read them."

"How did Marshall Watkins take to all that?" asked Mom.

"Oh, with boundless enthusiasm. I think he can believe in anything completely — if he sees a good magazine article in it, and I think he's marked down Mr. Whitney for one," said Dad. "Otherwise, I don't think he believes in much of anything."

After that, for a while, life settled down into a pleasant summer routine. When I wistfully admired Leo's tent and hinted around about how it must be great to sleep outside, he frowned and looked put upon and finally stalked off to the barn without a word. He returned with his old pup tent, which unbeknownst to me had been stored in the loft. He showed me how to pitch it on the other side of the lawn, not too close to his, and from then on I slept outside too.

One thing was clear, though: Leo's regard for my father was growing steadily. Listening to him talk to Dad, I could just picture his precocious intellectual discussions with some of the teachers at his special school. I am sure he missed those sessions, but was finding a more than satisfactory substitute in my father's company. We three played a lot of catch and went to the town beach together every day for a swim, and at times I got pretty fed up with all the brainy talk.

Mom, who had a way of not missing anything, finally had to have a little talk with *me*. It all had to do with the fact that Leo didn't have any father, and missed one whether he consciously knew it or not, so that it was only natural and right for him to find a partial substitute in an uncle. I was lucky enough to have a father, so surely I should not mind sharing him for a little while with someone who did not have one, etc., etc.

It was all pretty obvious stuff, but like a lot of obvious stuff it worked. Now that I could feel sorry for Leo, I no longer minded it so much when he talked over my head to my father.

Dad even talked to us about the book he was working on. I was there, that is, though really he was talking more to Leo, who could understand more than I did — but by then I had had my session with Mom and could tolerate it all with a new feeling of security. But at any rate, Leo grew so interested that Dad even began to read us bits from the old letters and papers and articles he was researching.

And that is how we happened to find out about O.S. and N.S.

One evening about six-thirty, just after supper, we had gone up with Dad to his workroom because he had something to read to us that he had come across during the day. He was smart enough, by the way — probably coached by Mom — never to exclude me from any of his talks with Leo, even though a lot of it might be hard for me to understand.

This time he began to read an article which gave the date as "Dec. 2, 1714 (O.S.)."

I asked the fateful question. I'm sure Leo would have, but I happened to get it out first.

"What's O.S., Dad?"

"O.S.? Well, that means the date given is Old Style,

before the calendar was reformed. N.S. means New Style."

"What's the difference?"

Dad was a great one for looking up things. He never believed in guesswork if a good reference book was at hand. Aunt Fanny had let him bring the twenty-four volumes of her old encyclopedia up to his workroom. He reached for the volume labeled "BRAI to CAS" and found the article — "Calendars."

The gist of what he read us was this:

The early Romans had a twelve-month calendar that was sort of like ours, only it did not take into account the fact that the year is not exactly 365 days long, but actually almost 365¼ days long.

By the time of Julius Caesar, that few extra hours a year had gotten the calendar out of whack. January was coming in the fall instead of in the winter. So Julius Caesar tried to fix it up, and did a pretty good job. He took care of the extra quarter of a day by making every fourth year a leap year, giving an extra day to February just as we do now.

The new calendar was called the Julian calendar, and most of Europe used it for the next 1600 years or so.

That quarter of a day was not an exact 6-hour quarter, however, but really 5 hours, 48 minutes, and about 46 seconds. So after another 1600 years the calendar was out of whack again.

By then it was ten days off. This time Pope Gregory the Great fixed it up. From that time on a leap year has been skipped in the first year of centuries that cannot be divided by 400. The years 1700, 1800, and 1900 were not leap years. The year 2000 will be.

Those ten extra days still had to be taken care of somehow, though, so in the year 1582 Pope Gregory dropped ten days out of the month of October. The day after October 4 became October 15.

England, however, was a Protestant country, so England was slow about making the change. It took England nearly two centuries to admit that Pope Gregory's calendar was correct, and to switch to it from the Julian calendar.

By that time the Julian calendar was eleven days off. In 1752, then, eleven days were dropped out of the English calendar to make it correspond to the Gregorian calendar.

British workmen, who did not understand this, got very mad about it. There were riots, and workers went around shouting, "Give us back our eleven days!" But finally things settled down and the calendar was accepted.

In America, George Washington changed his birthday. He was born on February 11, 1732, Old Style, but when he was twenty and the calendar was changed he added eleven days, and from then on he celebrated his birthday on February 22, New Style.

At this point in Dad's reading from the encyclopedia, two things happened.

One of them happened to me. Something far in the back of my mind began to stir.

The other thing happened to Leo. He sat up and almost shouted:

"Wait a minute, Uncle Paul! Did you say they changed the calendar in seventeen hundred and fifty-two?"

The Captain Butcher episode was a thing of the past. For over a week I had not given it another thought, and I doubt if Dad had, either. But Leo's reaction showed that he had never quite put it out of his mind.

"July eleventh, seventeen forty-six . . ."

Leo was muttering the date with a wild look in his eyes, and by that time Dad's face had changed expression too.

"You're right! Leo, you're right. By eighteen forty-six it's very likely the people here on the island didn't think about the fact that the date a hundred years earlier was Old Style. Historians often disregard it even today, because as a rule the few days' difference is of no significance . . . Come to think of it, it's the same difference as Washington's Birthday. February eleventh, February twenty-second . . . July eleventh, July twenty-second —"

Leo's burning eyes were on the calendar.

"And today is the twenty-third!"

To make a discovery like that, only to find you have made it one day too late! This was the most frustrating moment of our young lives. Last night, then, had been the real anniversary of Captain Butcher's crime!

Leo was like someone who had been hit by a bullet. At first he was only stunned. It took a few seconds for the pain to come.

"We could have been there! We could have been there last night, if only we had known!"

Even Dad was upset.

"I never thought about that calendar-change business," he said. "I mean, who would have?"

"Marshall Watkins should have, darn him!"

Leo, who had dropped angrily into an armchair, sprang up with such a wild cry you'd have thought an upholstery pin was lurking in the slipcover seat.

"Wait a minute!" he yammered. "Those two boys! Remember what Watkins said about the two boys who came running home — what did he say? 'A week or so later' — came running home a week or so later saying they had seen ghosts on the beach? Oh, that dope! Marshall Watkins had the clue right under his nose and was too stupid to see it!"

"So were we," Dad pointed out, and then had the good grace to add, "or at least I was. You boys didn't know about the calendar change."

Marshall Watkins's book was still on his worktable. He picked it up and riffled through the pages, finding the place he wanted.

"Here. Here's what he says. 'A week or so later, two young boys came running home one evening full of a story of having seen ghosts on the beach — "one murthering t'other!" — but on close questioning they finally admitted they had not been near Butcher's Cove at all, but rather at an inlet a mile away along the shore.' "

He looked up from the book.

"East Inlet, that would be . . ."

"Yes! And the other tower is there — East Light! It all fits! Instead of burying his box right there on the beach in the cove —"

"He took an extra precaution," said Dad, getting a little excited himself. "He went a mile up the beach to East Inlet and buried it there, so that even Jabez Tompkins wouldn't have too accurate an idea of its location. Then later, when he told his story, that's one thing he kept to himself, so that no one could ever find Tompkins's grave."

"And Tompkins didn't know the true location of the jewel box until he saw that map Butcher showed him!" A study in misery, Leo collapsed into the chair again. "And last night —"

"Now, Leo, take it easy." Dad tried to ease the pain with a little reasonable talk. "We're still only guessing. And — well, I'm sure you didn't miss anything. Let's face it, in spite of the story those two boys told —"

Hunched in the depths of the armchair, Leo glared up at him.

"Maybe. Maybe nothing happened. But now we'll never know. And we could have *been* there, without any crowd, all alone . . ."

Well, there was nothing could be done about it now. If anything had happened on the beach at East Inlet last night, we had missed it. There was nothing we could do now to turn back the clock. But even then Leo could not stop twisting the knife in the wound.

"No wonder nobody felt anything that night at Butcher's Cove!" he groaned. "Nothing ever happened there!"

As I said before, we had eaten supper and it was now about seven-thirty. Leo sent a tortured glance out the window. Ours was one of those excruciating disappointments that make it hard for the victims to sit still. He had to do something. When he told us his plan I was all for it. It sounded like the only possible release for our feelings.

"I'm going to ride out there," he said. "I'm at least going to see the place and — and look around."

"Me, too!"

He gave me a gloomy glance, but didn't say no. Then we all stared at each other for a moment, and finally Dad nodded.

"Get it out of your system, boys," he said. "You'll feel better."

Eleven

At first Leo pedaled along so furiously I could not keep up with him.

"Hey, Leo! Wait for me!"

He shot a vacant glare back over his shoulder and kept going. It wasn't that he was trying to get away from me or even trying to hurry. He was merely working off some of the misery that was gnawing at the pit of his stomach. After a while he slowed down and I was able to catch up with him.

The words he greeted me with showed how his mind was working.

"We could have had the place to ourselves!"

I kept quiet. There was nothing left to say. For that matter, I had my own preoccupations. Something was still eating at *me,* something I could not put my finger on yet . . .

They say we never really forget anything we have ever known or experienced. It is all there, somewhere in that miraculous storage and retrieval system that is the human brain. It is all there — if we can just get at it.

Well, something was certainly stirring in the back of *my* mind, but for the moment it consisted of nothing more than an uneasy feeling, a feeling there was something I had once heard that I now needed very much to remember. It had to do with what Dad had been reading to us, but what was it? What —

The man on the boat! Suddenly I was seeing him again, and suddenly I had moved a notch nearer to remembering, because now, like a double exposure, another memory had superimposed itself over the more recent one.

I was on a train with my father — a crowded subway train. There was one seat, and he made me sit down while he stood, hanging onto a strap. So I sat down, next to —

The old gentleman! The one who first said, "Hi, sonny! What's your name?" and I said, "George — and it's my birthday!" because I had been telling that to everyone I met, the way a little kid will.

My birthday. But what about my birthday? Leaning down toward me and speaking in quiet tones that somehow cut clearly through the noisy rattle and rumble of the subway train, he had told me something about my birthday, but try as I might I could not recall anything more. I wished I could talk to Leo about it, but how could I? It was all such a vague muddle, hardly something I could explain as we raced along on our bikes, especially with him in his present mood.

I gave up the struggle with memory and looked around me. At least we had better weather this time than we had that night at Butcher's Cove. There were clouds in the sky, but they were fleecy. Low and red in the west, the sun sent long spidery shadows racing ahead of us, as we spun along the road, and laid a shimmer of red gold across the peaceful moors. We had chosen the best possible medicine for a couple of bruised spirits. A summer evening like that one could not help but bring the philosopher out in anyone, even Leo. By the time we had reached the bend in the road where we had left our bikes to walk down to Butcher's Cove he was calmer. Glancing sideways at me as we went past, he managed to produce a sour grin.

"All those darn fools out here in the wrong place at the wrong time . . ."

"All those Doanes having their picnic," I said, and he actually snickered.

A quarter of a mile further the road climbed to a high point that brought the whole southern end of the island into view. We stopped and looked back, down toward Butcher's Cove. The scene was so peaceful it was insipid. Without saying a word we sent our eyes traveling along the shore to the southeast. Leo glanced at me and pointed.

"There it is. That's East Inlet. And there's East Light."

Still a long way off, but visible if you knew what to

look for, was the second stone tower; below it was an inlet smaller than Butcher's Cove but still a definite indentation in the shoreline.

"The real thing. And last night . . ."

Leo broke off. The subject was too painful.

"Well, come on. We can still get a lot closer on the road before we have to start walking."

In those days no one lived out in that part of the island. No one. We had it to ourselves.

The road finally left us with about the same distance to travel to East Inlet as the walk down to Butcher's Cove. We ditched our bikes by the road and set off. By now the sun was a red ball behind us that quickly dropped out of sight as we went down the long sweep of the moors toward the sea. In the hollows around us whippoorwills were beginning to call.

For a while we walked along in silence; we never knew exactly when it was that something drifted our way in the atmosphere that was like the scent of lions coming to the nostrils of antelope. A perfect soft summer night was settling around us, but that calm serenity was a lying mask. Why else should skin crawl and heart beat faster and breath come harder as though the air were suddenly heavy and turbulent with unseen forces?

If I could have told myself that I was letting my imagination run away with me, that would have been comforting. The frightening fact was that this gradual, insidious onslaught of uneasiness did not come from inside me but from outside. The impact was so marked as to seem almost physical. I turned to Leo and saw that he too had changed. He was walking with the wariness of an alarmed animal, and he was trembling, not so much with fear as with the bowstring tautness of heightened senses.

"Something *must* have happened here last night! It's still in the air."

Had I been older I probably would have responded with some grateful outburst such as, "Thank God! You feel it, too?" As it was, all I said was "Yes!" But the same thankfulness went into the single word. And it was Leo, surprised but fiercely glad to be supported, who said some of those other words.

"You feel it?"

"Yes!"

We stared at each other, and because at that early time in our lives neither of us, not even Leo, knew how to put into words the shadowy conceptions that filled our minds, neither of us said anything more. But the mind can ask questions without words, and both of our minds were asking the same ones:

Was it possible? Could a supernatural event, or a psychic disturbance, or anything you wanted to call it, leave a miasma of evil behind to linger in the atmosphere for a while, like the acrid smell after a bad fire? Had an echo of ancient violence, on a century-long wavelength, pulsated through this atmosphere the night before?

There was no need for words. We were afraid, and yet how could we be afraid of something that had already happened? We turned and walked on, and moments later we stood on the dunes above the inlet. Except for being smaller it was much like Butcher's Cove, but with one or two important differences. For one thing, the strip of beach itself was much smaller. For another —

"Look at that boulder!" Leo's voice was a hoarse whisper. "He could really get behind that one!"

At the eastern corner of the small beach, so close to the face of the dune that we had to walk to the edge to see it, stood a large jagged boulder. With careful, deliberate steps we moved down onto the beach and walked around, on the real scene at last, walking in the footsteps of Captain Butcher and Jabez Tompkins, walking over the very spot where . . . We stood staring down at the sand and the feeling persisted, the feeling of something hanging in the air, something unresolved. But why now, afterward? . . .

Leo glanced up as though his eyes had suddenly been attracted by something. The quick dart of my eyes followed his toward the tower. From the beach only the top part was visible.

"I thought . . ."

We exchanged a glance while he left his thought unsaid. He began to walk toward the tower, up the slope of the dune and across the spiky beach grass, and I knew from the stiff set of his legs that every step was an individual act of courage.

Watching him gave me just enough courage to follow.

Twelve

Walking toward the tower was like walking through a wall of gradually thickening cobwebs that remained invisible even as they strengthened. Cobwebs, or a dance of unseen particles gathering for some horrid purpose, an evil force pulsating there, somewhere within the tower — and all in a profound silence that trembled with overtones of coiled malignancy.

For a moment we stood paralyzed, staring inside while the powerful sensation increased, and then suffocating panic took us by the throat.

I have a confused memory of turning away and running blindly, fleeing from nothing I could name, yet finding myself a hundred frantic strides later sprawled on the rough grass in a hollow, panting and sweating, but safe — or at least unmolested by anything I could identify. And Leo was there close by. Belly down, we eyed each other like two frightened soldiers in one of those shellholes on a World War I battlefield.

Leo was beyond pretense now.

"I lost my head," he croaked, appalled by this successful assault on his self-discipline and courage. "I don't understand."

"No!"

"But you *felt* . . . something?"

"Yes!"

"What?"

"I don't know. It was just a feeling of, of — like something was *there!* Listen, Leo, you don't suppose . . ."

"What?"

"You don't suppose it *always* feels that way there?"

"It couldn't. Other people . . ."

"Well, yes. Someone would have . . ."

Leo turned over and sat up. He was still breathing hard, but he was regrouping his forces, reestablishing control.

"We'll come back tomorrow," he decided. "That's the only way to find out. And next time I'm not going to run, I swear I'm not! A haunted tower! I don't believe it! Not even Marshall Watkins talked about a haunted tower."

"But he had the wrong one anyway."

"Even so . . ."

"Then why —?"

"I don't know. It *must* have been us."

"I don't believe it! I wasn't just imagining things!"

"How do you know?"

"It wasn't all in my mind, I tell you! It was . . . it was *outside!* I don't know how to explain, but —"

"I felt it, too."

I stared at him, bewildered by his admission.

"Well, then. What more do you want?"

He stood up, stubborn and determined.

"It still could have been us. And that's what we've got to find out."

"*Now?*"

"No." Even Leo had his limits. "Tomorrow. Let's go home. If we get going now we might make it before it's pitch dark."

Here, at least, was a suggestion he did not have to sell me on. I was on my feet at once, churning up the slope of the little hollow that had sheltered us. I wanted to make a beeline for our bikes with never a backward glance. That, however, would have taken more self-control than I possessed. I could not keep my head from turning for a single, quick, furtive glimpse of the tower beside the inlet, the tower which had by now become a dark gray silhouette against fading bands of blue, pink, and violet sky. I looked, and my heart hit my chest like an inner fist.

"Leo!"

I pointed.

"Leo, I thought . . ."

He was staring, transfixed. And he nodded.

For a second or two the top of the tower had not

been a straight line. The line had been muddled part-way across by a dark bulky mass. A mass dark and bulky that could have been the shape of a man's head and shoulders. And now it was gone.

As I whirled around, ready to take off in blubbering panic, Leo caught me by the arm with a grip that flashed pain through me like a red flame. I cried out, but he held on mercilessly.

"No! If — if anything is in that tower it's going to stay there —"

"It's a real man!" I screamed. "Some nut —"

"Stop it! He's had all this time to come after us if he wanted to. He could have come down after us when we were right there. Only . . . Now, listen! It was probably a trick of the light."

"What do you mean?"

I made that a hysterical question full of total dis-belief, but Leo only gritted his teeth and shook me hard.

"I mean nobody is there! Now just start walking, and don't look back anymore, you hear?"

Everything he was saying was aimed only at getting me under control, of course, but at the same time he believed at least part of what he was saying: he be-lieved there was nothing or nobody in that tower that was going to come after us. At any rate it worked. When he let go of my arm I walked. Rubbing my arm, wincing at the bruise, I walked.

Had anyone asked me, I would have sworn that in my state of mind at that moment I was unable to think of anything except putting distance between us and that terrible tower. Yet all the time, even then, a part of my mind must have continued its own frenzied pursuit of an elusive memory like a fox after a hare, knowing it was something important that should be brought back to the surface.

Yes, that must have been it. Because just as we finally reached our bikes, with the dusk so deep that darkness was only minutes away, and when my only conscious thought was concerned with how great it was going to feel to jump on my bike and start burning up the road back toward Aunt Fanny's house . . .

"George, what's the matter?"

"Wait!"

Something was struggling to break through the final barrier between consciousness and "forgotten" memories.

It came at last.

"George Washington!"

I shouted the illustrious name so suddenly that Leo nearly dropped his bike.

"I remember now! I was a little kid and it was my birthday," I babbled, "and this old man on the subway told me I was very lucky because I was born on George Washington's *real* birthday!"

"Are you cracking up?" cried Leo. I was counting on my fingers, counting to see if it really could be true.

"Yes!"

"*What?*"

"No! I mean — listen, Leo! Remember what those workmen said? 'Give us back our eleven days'?"

Leo's mind worked fast, but to have something like that thrown at him out of the blue was bewildering. And before he could think of anything to say, I went on.

"The English dropped eleven days out of their calendar. The *twelfth* day was the next day! This old man I met told me — George Washington did it wrong! He added eleven to eleven, but that doesn't take away enough days! Count them up for yourself. Instead of having his birthday on the eleventh he had it on the twenty-second — but there are only *ten* days between the eleventh and the twenty-second!"

Holding up my hands I counted them off on my trembling fingers.

"Twelve, thirteen, fourteen, fifteen, sixteen, seventeen, eighteen, nineteen, twenty, twenty-one — ten days!"

I added the final touch.

"George Washington's new birthday should have been the twenty-third, the same as mine! *That* is what he told me!"

Leo's face had gone white. His mouth opened and closed, opened and closed, but nothing came out. Double-checking me, he began counting on his fingers, too. Then he began to croak out the last few numbers.

"Eighteen, nineteen, twenty, twenty-one — you're right! And if February eleventh should be February twenty-third, then July eleventh would be . . ."

"Today! Now!"

For a moment Leo did not move. Then he tipped his bike on its side.

"I'm going back."

Can you understand how I could have been terrified only minutes earlier and yet turn back with him now?

Everything was clear now, all we had felt, all we had seen. We were drawn back by needs within us that went beyond fear. We had to know, and if we ran recklessly it was because we were afraid we would be too late.

We had cats' eyes in the dark, and a good thing, too. Here and there bare patches of gleaming sandy soil threw back light to help. At first we could see nothing ahead but the mere outlines of moors and dunes and inlet, with the horizon lost in the dark sea and sky beyond them. But then Leo skidded to a stop, grabbed my shoulder, and pointed.

Far ahead of us a dim blob of light was moving steadily toward the inlet.

Thirteen

$\mathbf{J}$abez. Jabez Tompkins."

I remember how calm Leo's voice had become when he spoke the name, and how calmly I heard it. We were beyond any ordinary sense of fright, numbed by a dreamlike conviction of inevitability. Silently we watched the dim circle of light reach the edge of the dunes and disappear down the slope.

"He'll have to dig. It will take him a while. We'll get there in time," muttered Leo, and to me his mystical assurance seemed totally justified. We no longer hurried but walked steadily on, choosing our way without hesitation and without stumbles. Cats' eyes, yes, but that night all our senses seemed sharper than ever before or since. We learned then why men sometimes delight in danger. It is because nothing makes them feel more completely *alive*.

Leo spoke only once more. That was when the tower loomed up in the darkness to our right.

"He was there, watching and waiting, but by now he's not there anymore," he whispered with the certainty of prescience.

We traveled the last few yards on our hands and knees and then our bellies, inching our way toward the edge of the dunes above the beach. And then finally, slowly, we raised our heads to look down.

A lantern, or the image of a lantern, sat on the beach, and the light it cast was more like phosphorescence than anything made by a flame. It seemed to give a blurry glow to the figure that strained forward over a gaping pit in the sand — or did the figure have a glow of its own? The spade it held was knifing into the sand, scooping out spadeful after spadeful. Yet not a sound was to be heard; not the gritting of sand against sand, not the spattering of sand flung aside, not the baffled curses of a mouth that was moving in a lividly shining face.

Then all at once bafflement was over, digging stopped. The spade was flung aside. The glowing figure dropped to its knees with its back toward us and scrabbled with both hands in the sand, then staggered to its feet holding a small box.

Below us, something else moved.

A dark mass flickered into view as we strained forward to peer down at the jagged boulder. We could see a dark arm extended, and the dull gleam of an iron barrel pointed straight at the figure holding the box as it turned.

We saw a pair of fiery eyes widen in a nightmarish contortion of a face as the box tumbled onto the sand, fumbled by the writhing hands. We saw a noiseless flash of flame from the pistol barrel, and then we saw two horrible holes.

One black hole was a mouth opened as though in a scream. The other was a smaller black hole just above the staring eyes.

And then the scene vanished into darkness.

How long did I lie there on the edge of the dune with my face pressed into the bristly beach grass, too paralyzed to move a muscle? An instant. An eternity.

"It's over."

Leo's incredible tone of voice shocked me back into life. There was not the slightest tinge of fear in it. He *knew* there was nothing left to be afraid of.

And he was pulling loose the flashlight clipped onto his belt!

It had a new bulb in it now and this time it worked. He shone it on the beach below us.

Nothing marred the smooth surface of the beach but a crisscross of footprints.

Our footprints.

Fourteen

We went home with our story — and Dad demolished it.

He was a better mathematician than we were.

He listened to us with a grave face, began counting on his own fingers, and shook his head gently.

"No."

"No? What do you mean, no?"

"You're forgetting something. You have to *replace* the eleventh with the twenty-second, right?"

We stared at him, stomachs knotting with a premonition of disaster.

"So you have to count the eleventh as one of the days you take away."

That was it: 11, 12, 13, 14, 15, 16, 17, 18, 19, 20, 21 — eleven days.

"The twenty-second now follows the tenth, taking

the place of the old eleventh," Dad explained, looking down with compassion at our stricken faces. "George, I'm sure your old gentleman meant well, but he was probably like a lot of old people who get a pet theory. Nothing can convince them they are wrong. But I am afraid he *was* wrong, and George Washington was right.

"I remember now, too. I had taken you to the zoo while your mother and the twins got everything ready for your birthday party. I couldn't hear what the old man was telling you, and when you tried to tell me after we got off the subway I couldn't get it straight — it was pretty complicated stuff for a six-year-old to repeat. You were still trying when we got home, but then the excitement of your birthday party made you forget everything else. I — I wish I had understood you then. I might have saved you both a lot of pain now."

We were shattered. There was no getting around it: Washington had not made a mistake after all. Our "proof" lay in ruins. We were left with no defense against the various explanations for our experience that naturally sprang to Dad's mind. His preference among those explanations was for some form of auto-hypnotism or mass hypnotism, if two boys could be called a mass.

"You were pretty well worked up by the time you reached the inlet the first time. By the time you left you had convinced yourselves there was something strange about the atmosphere. Then, at a perfect psychological moment, just as you were about to start home, George remembered what the old gentleman told him. That's amazing, too, George, because you were only six years old the year I took you to the zoo.

"So now George remembers what the old gentleman told him, and you're both convinced that tonight was the true night the ghosts would return. You start back to the beach, and partway back you think you see a dim light moving down across the moors. In that state of mind, alone in a deserted spot in the darkness, you are ready to hallucinate almost anything. You now 'see' what you have convinced yourselves you will see.

"And don't think I'm blaming you, because I'm not. If I had been there and could have believed as sincerely as you did that the correct night was tonight and not last night, I'm sure I would have thought I saw what you saw, and there would now be three of us swearing to it."

In other words, he tried to be as nice about it as he could. But the effect on both of us was still a shattering one. We felt we had somehow been tricked, cheated, swindled. I thought some terrible things about that well-meaning but misguided old gentleman I had met so long ago. Was it true that everything we believed we had seen and experienced that night was merely some kind of hallucination? Were we only a couple of silly, hysterical kids?

As exhausted as we were, neither of us slept well that night. It was hardly dawn when Leo came prowling over to see if I was awake. We went back to his tent and with gray, drawn faces sat talking it over.

Leo's stubborn mind was still battling against all odds.

"I don't understand it. I don't know why it all happened one night later than it should have, but I know what I saw, and you saw it, too. Nobody will ever believe us, and I'll never tell another living soul — but we know!"

"I guess so," I said wearily. "But why did that date have to be wrong! Darn it, why does George Washington always have to be right?"

That might have been the end of it, had it not been for a bulky packet Dad brought home from the post office later in the morning. He called to us on his way into the house and stopped on the porch to show us what he had received.

"I told you Mr. Whitney was a nice old fellow," he said, detaching a letter from a sheaf of photostated pages. "Come on up to my room and let's see what he has to say."

Leo responded with a glum frown and a shrug, anything but eager to have a painful subject reopened. But he came upstairs with us to Dad's workroom and listened grimly while Dad, sitting behind his worktable, read the letter:

Dear Mr. Crowell:

You expressed interest in the original account of Captain Butcher's story written by the warder, Edmund Higby. Here is my copy of it, which I would appreciate your returning to me when you have finished with it.

Also enclosed is a copy of a letter which I have

just received from a descendant of the Wycroft family, and which has left me quite annoyed, particularly with the slipshod methods of a writer such as Mr. Watkins, who, one can plainly see now, never digs deeply enough into any subject he takes up.

The letter, written by Captain Wycroft to his sister, gives me strong reason to suspect we were all present at Butcher's Cove on the wrong date entirely . . .

"He's caught on to the Old Style–New Style mistake," said Leo, and Dad nodded.

"It's just too bad he didn't do it sooner!"

"Well, anyway, I'll bet Watkins won't get any article out of Mr. Whitney *now,*" said Leo, and looked fiercely pleased at the thought.

"I'll bet not," agreed Dad, and resumed his reading of the letter:

According to Higby's account, Butcher recollected the date of the murder as July 11. In his letter, however (and I am more inclined to trust a former naval captain, with his ingrained habits of accuracy in such matters, than a man such as Butcher had become), Wycroft gives the date as July 12 . . .

That was as far as Dad got with his reading.

For a moment he sat staring at the letter. The pages were trembling in his hand. Leo had sprung to his feet.

Like someone possessed he leaned forward with his hands flat on the tabletop, his eyes burning down at Dad.

"Well, Uncle Paul?" His voice was little more than a harsh whisper. "What do you say now?"

My father's face was white. The comfortable beliefs of a lifetime were deserting him. He looked up at Leo and gave him an honest answer.

"Now," he said, "I don't know what to think."

Many years from now, in the year 2046, on a night late in July, when the last glimmer of light is fading from the summer sky, will two other boys find themselves near the inlet at the southeastern reach of Broadmoor Island, walking toward the ancient stone tower and the strip of beach? . . .